"We Don't Have A Relationship. We Simply Share An Address And A Bed, When The Mood Strikes You."

Clayton slammed his fist against the railing, then whirled to face Rena. "Haven't I provided you with a home, seen that you and the kids have everything you need, everything you could possibly want? What the hell is it you expect from me?"

Rena stared at him, her eyes filling with tears. Then she dragged the back of her hand across her cheek and gave her chin a lift. "Nothing," she said and turned for the door. "Absolutely nothing."

Something in her voice—a certainty of purpose, a calmness despite the earlier storm—chilled Clayton to the bone. This wasn't some dramatic stunt she was pulling in order to get his attention. She really intended to leave him!

But Clayton wasn't a four-time rodeo world champion for nothing. He knew how to win his heart's desire…and his heart had never desired anything more than his wife….

The toughest men in Texas
are about to be tamed!

Dear Reader,

As we celebrate Silhouette's 20th anniversary year as a romance publisher, we invite you to welcome in the fall season with our latest six powerful, passionate, provocative love stories from Silhouette Desire!

In September's MAN OF THE MONTH, fabulous Peggy Moreland offers a *Slow Waltz Across Texas*. In order to win his wife back, a rugged Texas cowboy must learn to let love into his heart. Popular author Jennifer Greene delivers a special treat for you with *Rock Solid,* which is part of the highly sensual Desire promotion, BODY & SOUL.

Maureen Child's exciting miniseries, BACHELOR BATTALION, continues with *The Next Santini Bride,* a responsible single mom who cuts loose with a handsome Marine. The next installment of the provocative Desire miniseries FORTUNE'S CHILDREN: THE GROOMS is *Mail-Order Cinderella* by Kathryn Jensen, in which a plain-Jane librarian seeks a husband through a matchmaking service and winds up with a Fortune! Ryanne Corey returns to Desire with a *Lady with a Past,* whose true love woos her with a chocolate picnic. And a nurse loses her virginity to a doctor in a night of passion, only to find out the next day that her lover is her new boss, in *Doctor for Keeps* by Kristi Gold.

Be sure to indulge yourself this autumn by reading all six of these tantalizing titles from Silhouette Desire!

Enjoy!

Joan Marlow Golan

Joan Marlow Golan
Senior Editor, Silhouette Desire

Please address questions and book requests to:
Silhouette Reader Service
U.S.: 3010 Walden Ave., P.O. Box 1325, Buffalo, NY 14269
Canadian: P.O. Box 609, Fort Erie, Ont. L2A 5X3

Slow Waltz
Across Texas
PEGGY MORELAND

Silhouette®

Desire

Published by Silhouette Books
America's Publisher of Contemporary Romance

Knowing that I've entertained a reader or fulfilled a reader's expectations is what makes the hours of sitting in front of a computer monitor worthwhile. I'd like to dedicate this book to four readers who have always taken the time to write and tell me that they've enjoyed my stories: Daisella Vann, Bonnie Hendricks, Kathleen Stone and Christy Jenkins. Thank you, ladies, for the kind words, the unflagging support and the encouragement you've offered throughout the years.

 SILHOUETTE BOOKS

ISBN 0-373-76315-8

SLOW WALTZ ACROSS TEXAS

Books by Peggy Moreland

Silhouette Desire

A Little Bit Country #515
Run for the Roses #598
Miss Prim #682
The Rescuer #765
Seven Year Itch #837
The Baby Doctor #867
Miss Lizzy's Legacy #921
A Willful Marriage #1024
**Marry Me, Cowboy* #1084
**A Little Texas Two-Step* #1090
**Lone Star Kind of Man* #1096
†*The Rancher's Spittin' Image* #1156
†*The Restless Virgin* #1163
†*A Sparkle in the Cowboy's Eyes* #1168
†*That McCloud Woman* #1227
Billionaire Bridegroom #1244
†*Hard Lovin' Man* #1270
‡*Ride a Wild Heart* #1306
‡*In Name Only* #1313
‡*Slow Waltz Across Texas* #1315

Silhouette Special Edition

Rugrats and Rawhide #1084

*Trouble in Texas
†Texas Brides
‡Texas Grooms

PEGGY MORELAND

published her first romance with Silhouette in 1989 and continues to delight readers with stories set in her home state of Texas. Winner of the National Readers' Choice Award, a nominee for the *Romantic Times Magazine* Reviewer's Choice Award and a finalist for the prestigious RITA Award, Peggy has appeared on the *USA Today* and Waldenbooks bestseller lists. When not writing, she enjoys spending time at the farm riding her quarter horse, Lo-Jump. She, her husband and three children make their home in Round Rock, Texas. You may write to Peggy at P.O. Box 2453, Round Rock, TX 78680-2453.

IT'S OUR 20th ANNIVERSARY!
We'll be celebrating all year,
Continuing with these fabulous titles,
On sale in September 2000.

One

He could see it, almost feel it, as he watched them.

He imagined calling out their names. *Hey, Brittany! Brandon!* His children turning to him, their eyes going wide, their surprise upon seeing their daddy quickly turning to excitement. They would run down the sidewalk, squealing, their chunky little legs churning, their tiny arms flung wide in welcome. Laughing, he would scoop them up in a big bear hug and swing them around and around until they were all three dizzy.

He could see it. Almost feel it.

Almost.

But a fear learned at an early age of exposing his feelings and being rejected kept Clayton from putting the scene he envisioned to the test.

Instead he strode across the street to the park where the twins played, his hands shoved deeply into his pockets, his expression shadowed by his cowboy hat, his eyes—as well as his emotions—concealed behind dark aviator sunglasses. He came to a stop not six feet from the sandbox where the twins were carrying on a game of tug-of-war with a bright red sand bucket.

"My turn," four-year-old Brittany cried, giving the bucket a determined tug.

"No, mine," her twin brother, Brandon, argued stubbornly, and yanked right back.

The plastic sand bucket looked as if it would snap any minute from the pressure placed on it by two sets of warring hands.

"Can't you two share?"

Clayton didn't realize how gruffly he'd spoken the question until two little heads whipped around to peer up at him, two sets of brown eyes wide with fear. They released their holds on the bucket and the loss of tension sent both toppling over backward in opposite directions. He stooped and lifted them from the sand, tucking one under each arm, as if they were sacks of feed.

"Clayton! What do you think you're doing?"

He turned to see his wife charging across the park's carefully manicured grass toward him, her face flushed with anger. When had she cut her hair? he wondered in dismay. That beautiful blond mane. Gone.

Shocked by the dramatic change the new style made in her appearance, he let his gaze drift down her length, noting the body-hugging white T-shirt tucked into crisp khaki shorts, and the stretch of long, tanned legs. And when had she managed to lose that last ten, stubborn pounds she'd carried since the twins' birth? he asked himself. He tried to remember the last time he'd seen her. Had it been a month? Two? Or closer to three?

She reached him and snatched his daughter from his arms, her brown eyes dark with fury.

And that's when he noticed that her wedding ring was missing—the simple gold band he'd bought her in the jewelry store right down the street from the courthouse where they'd married. The shock he'd felt upon seeing the changes in her appearance quickly gave way to icy-cold dread.

Rena had never taken off her wedding band before. Not even when the twins were born. He could still remember her stubborn refusal to remove it when the nurses at the hospital had demanded she take it off before wheeling her into the delivery room. With the twins' birth imminent, a compromise had quickly been reached, and the nurses had wound surgical tape around the ring, sealing it against her finger.

Realizing the significance of the missing ring, Clayton swallowed hard and shifted his gaze to hers to find her still glaring at him.

She quickly shifted Brittany to her hip and reached for Brandon. But Clayton turned away, preventing her from taking his son from him, as well. He hefted the boy up into his arms, but kept his gaze on his wife. "Hello, Rena."

Her eyes narrowed in suspicion. "What are you doing here, Clayton?"

"I came to take my family back home where they belong."

Brittany clapped a palm against her mother's cheek and forced her face to hers. "Are we goin' home, Mommy?'' she asked, her eyes wide with hope.

Rena caught her daughter's hand in hers and pressed a kiss against the center of the tiny palm, before offering her a soft smile of regret. "No, darling."

Brittany pushed her lips out into a pout. "But I wanna go home."

"Me, too," Brandon complained, echoing his sister's sentiments.

Rena leaned over and lovingly brushed a lock of blond hair from her son's forehead. "But the ranch isn't our home any longer," she reminded him gently. "Remember? We're staying with Nonnie and Pawpaw for a few days, then we're moving to a home of our own."

Brandon slipped an arm around Clayton's neck. "But what about Daddy?" he asked uncertainly. "Isn't he going to move with us, too?"

Rena's gaze flicked to Clayton's, then quickly back to her son's. "No, sweetheart," she said gently, though Clayton was sure he heard a quaver in her voice. "Daddy's home is at the ranch."

Brittany thrust out her lower lip and turned to look at her father. "But the ranch is our home, too, isn't it, Daddy?"

Clayton cleared his throat, not sure he could work a sound past the emotion that tightened his throat. "It sure is, baby."

Rena snapped her gaze to his, and he could see the anger, the resentment in the brown depths. "Don't make this any harder than it already is, Clayton," she warned in a low voice.

He lifted a shoulder. "You're the one who uprooted the kids. Not me."

Brittany's hand pressed against her mother's cheek again, turning her face to hers. "What's uprooted mean, Mommy?"

Forcing a smile for her daughter's sake, Rena tickled Brittany's tummy, making her giggle. "It means I dug you up out of the dirt like I would a tree," she teased, then swung her daughter up high in the air, making her squeal.

"Do *me*, Mommy!" Brandon cried, stretching his arms out to his mother. Rena took him from Clayton and wrapped her arms around both her children, clutching them to her breasts. She spun in a fast, dizzying circle, until all three collapsed onto the soft grass in a tangle of legs and arms, laughing.

Clayton tucked his own empty hands beneath his armpits and watched his wife and children roll around on the grass, feeling like a kid with his nose pressed up against the candy store window, with no means to purchase the sweets displayed inside. He wanted so badly to join them, to romp and play with them on the sweet-smelling grass.

But a lifetime of suppressing his feelings, of standing on the sidelines and wishing, his heart near bursting with the need to feel loved, to feel a part of a family, kept Clayton's boots glued to that spot of grass where he stood, his hands, empty and aching, still tucked tightly beneath his armpits.

Clayton stood on the patio of his in-laws' house, his hands shoved deeply into his pockets, staring up at the dark sky. The night was unseasonably cool, but he preferred the chill in the air to the frigid looks he received inside the house. His in-laws didn't care for him. Never had. But then, he didn't care much for them, either.

With a weary sigh, he dropped his chin to his chest and settled his gaze on the toe of his boot as he chipped at the patio's gray slate surface. He supposed he could understand their coolness. They'd had big plans for their only daughter. A life of luxury and refinement much like their own.

And she'd gone off and gotten herself knocked up by some rodeo cowboy.

Yeah, he thought, his sigh heavier this time as he turned his gaze up to the moon. He supposed he could understand the Palmers' dislike for him.

The French door behind him opened, and he tensed as he listened to the soft tread of footsteps approaching. He knew without looking it was Rena. The scent of her reached him first, and he inhaled deeply, quietly, savoring it. Lord, but he loved the smell of her. Sweet. Feminine. Seductive.

She came to a stop beside him and tipped her face up to the stars, hugging her arms tightly beneath her breasts. "It's cold out here," she said with a shiver.

Clayton glanced her way, then shrugged out of his jacket and turned to drape it around her shoulders. She looked up at him in surprise at the gesture, then slowly caught the lapels of the jacket and pulled them around her. He wasn't sure if it was the suddenness of his movement or the kindness in the act that drew her surprised look. But he wouldn't ask. He never did. He'd learned years ago never to question. The answers almost always ended up hurting.

When the silence continued to stretch between them, she turned her face away, her mouth dipping into a frown as if he'd disappointed her somehow. Stifling yet another sigh, Clayton turned his gaze back to the sky. They stood side by side though not touching, both staring at the dark star-studded sky. Minutes ticked by, the silence growing heavier and heavier between them.

"Clayton, I—"

"Rena, I—"

They spoke simultaneously, their words tangling. They glanced at each other, then away again, both pressing their lips together in annoyance.

"Go ahead," Clayton said gruffly. "You first."

Rena gave her chin a stubborn lift. "No, you," she insisted. "I've had my say."

Clayton angled his head to look at her, his eyes wide. "You've had your say?" he repeated. "A voice mail message telling me that you're leaving me and taking the kids with you is *all* you have to say to me after more than four years of marriage?"

She pulled the jacket more closely around her, refusing to look at him. "It's more than you've had to say to me in months."

He brought his hands to his hips as he glared down at her. "Maybe so, but *I* wasn't planning on leaving *you*," he said, first thrusting his thumb against his chest, then leveling an accusing finger at her. "And if I was, I sure as hell would've given you more warning than a lousy voice mail message."

Infuriated that he would assume the part of the injured party in their relationship, Rena whirled on him. "And what kind of warning would you have liked, Clayton? Would you have preferred that I'd kicked and screamed and thrown temper tantrums, demanding that you come home so that I could tell you in person that I was leaving you?''

"You're not that kind of woman. You don't throw fits. Never have.''

Her eyes blazed with newfound fury. "And how would *you* know what kind of woman I am? You were always off at another rodeo and never stayed around long enough to find out.'' She gave his chest a push and, off balance, he stumbled back a step. She surged forward. "But then, maybe you would have preferred that I loaded up the kids and chased you across the country so that I could tell you face-to-face that I was leaving you. Maybe you would have enjoyed a more public scene than the privacy of a voice mail message.''

When she reached out to give him another angry shove, he stood his ground and grabbed her hand, capturing it in his. "I didn't expect you do anything but stay at home where you belong.''

"Where I belong?'' she repeated incredulously, then wrenched free of his grasp and planted her hands on her hips. "I'm not some *cow,* that you can stick in a pasture and expect to stay put while you go off and do whatever it is you do when you're gone. I'm a woman, and I have feelings, needs. I—''

She felt the tears coming and clamped her lips tightly together, refusing to give in to them. When she was sure she had them under control, that she wouldn't humiliate herself by crying in front of him, she dropped her hands to her sides in defeat. "You don't care anything for me, Clayton. You never did.''

"I married you, didn't I! I gave those kids my name.''

She staggered back a step as if he'd struck her, the blood draining from her face.

Realizing too late that he'd hurt her with the carelessly spoken words, he dropped down onto one of the patio chairs and, groaning, buried his face in his hands. He dug the heels of his hands into his forehead, then slowly raked his fingers up through his hair as he lifted his face to look at her. "I didn't mean that the way it sounded, Rena."

"Yes, Clayton," she whispered, unable to keep the tremble, the hurt, from her voice, "I think you did. For the first time in your life, I think you said exactly what you feel." Flinging off his jacket, she turned on her heel and strode for the patio door, slamming it behind her.

Rather than ask Rena's parents for permission to stay in their guest bedroom so that he could be near his wife and kids, Clayton settled his horse in a stall at a boarding facility he'd used once before on a trip to Oklahoma, then checked himself into a motel on the edge of town. The accommodations weren't anything fancy, nothing like the guest bedroom in the Palmers' home with its canopied bed and luxurious private bath. But the sparse motel room had one thing going for it. He could rest there, knowing that there wouldn't be anyone around watching his every move, analyzing his every word and finding him lacking.

Feeling the frustration rising again, he shrugged off his jacket, then dropped down on the bed and yanked the jacket across his spread knees.

I married you, didn't I? I gave those kids my name.

Bracing his elbows on his thighs, he dragged his

hands slowly down his face, groaning, as he remembered his words to his wife. Why was it that, lately, every time he opened his mouth around Rena, it seemed he stuck his foot in it?

He propped his chin on his fists and stared at the bare wall opposite him. He didn't have an answer to the question. Hell, he thought, surging to his feet and tossing the jacket aside. He didn't have any answers at all. He paced the length of the room and back, a hand cupped around the base of his neck, massaging at the tension there.

The voice mail she'd left him informing him that she was leaving him had come as a shock. But that blow hadn't been anything compared to the one he'd received when he'd returned to their ranch and discovered Rena and the kids were already gone.

He stopped in front of the door and gulped back a sob, hearing again the eerie silence that had greeted him when he'd stepped inside the house, the hollow echo of his footsteps in rooms once filled with his children's furniture and toys, the squeal of their laughter.

Rena had been right, he admitted miserably, in saying he'd never been around much. Riding the rodeo circuit left little time for visits home. But in spite of his absences he'd always found comfort in knowing that his home was there for him, as were Rena and the kids, waiting for his return. And for a man who had never had a home or a family, the ranch had provided a sense of security he'd desperately needed.

A security it appeared he was about to lose.

He couldn't lose his home and family, he told himself, feeling the panic squeezing at his chest, the loss

already weighing heavy on his heart. He couldn't.
Rena and the kids meant everything to him. They
were his life, his reason for living.

Without them he was nothing.

Nothing.

Rena lay on her side, her knees drawn to her chest,
a corner of the sheet pressed tightly against her lips.
Hot, silent tears saturated the pillow beneath her
cheek.

She'd done the right thing, she told herself. She'd
had to leave Clayton. She couldn't go on living with
him the way things were and continue to pretend that
nothing was wrong. Not with him gone all the time
and her left alone on the ranch with the children.

Not without his love to keep her company during
the long, lonely nights when he was away.

She felt a sob rising and pressed the sheet more
tightly against her lips to choke it back.

He didn't love her. He couldn't. If he did, he
would come home more often, would want to spend
more time with her and the twins. As it was, he was
gone weeks at a time, never even bothering to call
and check on her or their children. And even when
he was at home, she reminded herself tearfully, he
wasn't there, at least not emotionally. Not for her.

When he was at the ranch, which seemed to occur
less and less frequently, he took care of what business needed his attention, then he'd leave again. And
while he was there, he never looked at her, never
talked to her, nor did he ever listen when she tried
to talk to him.

And he never touched her anymore…except when
they were in bed.

As a result, she felt empty inside, drained, as if she were a well that was drawn from time and time again, but with no one to replenish her emotional supply. She was dry, empty and felt as if she had nothing left to offer those who needed her most. Her children.

She rolled to her back, clutching the sheet to her breasts, and stared at the shadows dancing on the ceiling overhead. Was it so wrong to want Clayton's attention? she asked herself. To need it? To even demand it? She was his wife, after all, and there was no one else to give her the things she needed. And that realization was what had finally pushed her into leaving him, she knew.

She had no one.

Yet she still had needs.

She felt the familiar ache in her breasts beneath the weight of her arms. How long had it been since he had touched her there? Swept his tongue across her nipples? Suckled at her breasts? How long since he had lain with her, the heat of his body warming hers, his comforting weight pressing her more deeply into the bed they shared so rarely? How long since he'd buried himself in her? Filled her with his seed?

The ache spread, throbbing to life between her legs. Biting back a sob, she rolled to her side again.

Yes, she thought as the tears scalded her throat.

Rena Rankin still had needs.

Stretched out on one of the cushioned lounge chairs beside her parents' pool, Rena crossed her legs at the ankles and took a sip of her lemonade.

"So, are you going home with him?"

Rena shook her head at her friend Megan's question, then set her glass of lemonade on the wrought-iron table between them. "No, that wouldn't solve anything."

Megan drew back, looking at Rena in dismay. "Surely you aren't planning on staying here with your parents?"

Rena cast a glance over her shoulder at the stately two-story mansion behind them with its glistening mullioned windows, the long stretch of French doors that lined the curved patio, the carefully manicured shrubs that hugged the mauve stone walls and the urns spilling with brightly colored flowers, which changed almost magically with the seasons. Wealth. Perfection. Success. Those were the images her parents' home drew; the same images to which they had tried to make their only daughter conform. The same images she'd wanted so desperately to escape as a young, single woman. With a shudder she glanced away. "No, not permanently. Just for a few days."

Megan stretched out a hand and took Rena's, squeezing it within her own. "Oh, Rena," she murmured, her eyes filled with concern, "are you sure you know what you're doing?"

"Honestly?" At Megan's earnest nod, Rena sighed and withdrew her hand from her friend's. She pressed her head back against the plump cushions and stared blindly up at the clouds floating across the sky overhead. "No, but I can't go on living with Clayton. Not with the way things are between us."

"But you love Clayton! I know you do."

Rena lifted a shoulder. "I thought I did. But now...I'm not sure anymore."

"Of course you love him! And he loves you!"

"No, he doesn't."

"How do you know that? Has he told you that he doesn't?"

Rena snorted indelicately. "No, but Clayton rarely says anything. Or at least, not to me."

"Then you can't possibly know that he doesn't love you."

Rena turned her head slowly to peer at Megan through the dark sunglasses that concealed eyes swollen from a night spent crying over that very actuality. "Trust me," she replied dryly. "I know."

Megan huffed a breath and flopped back against the cushions, folding her arms stubbornly beneath her breasts. "Well, I think he does."

Rena sputtered a laugh. "And why would you think that? You haven't been around Clayton or talked to him in years."

"I was there the night you met him," Megan reminded her. "Remember?"

Rena turned her face away. "Yes, I remember."

"And do you also remember how you two just seemed to click?" she asked, snapping two fingers together for emphasis. "I've never seen chemistry like that before, nor have I since."

Rena fluttered a hand, dismissing her friend's opinion. "Lust. Pure and simple."

Megan jackknifed to a sitting position. "It was not just lust!" she cried, then clamped her lips together and stole a quick glance at the house to make sure that no one had overheard her. Though no faces appeared in any of the windows, she lowered her voice, obviously concerned that Rena's mother was hovering on the other side of the doors, as she had when they were teenagers, eavesdropping on their conversation. "Two star-crossed lovers destined to meet," she whispered furiously to Rena. "That's what the two of you were. One look from Clayton, one touch, and you came alive."

Even as her friend described the event, Rena felt the leap of nerves beneath her skin, the quickening of her breath, the heat racing through her veins. She could see Clayton as he'd stood that night, alone at the edge of the dance floor, his hands braced low on his hips. The sleeves of his black Western shirt had been rolled to his elbows, exposing muscled forearms dusted with dark hair, and his black cowboy hat had been shoved back on his head, revealing the sharp angles of an incredibly handsome face.

Black. The bad guys always wear black, she remembered thinking at the time, even as she'd smiled flirtatiously at him when he'd looked her way.

Furious with herself for even thinking about Clayton and the night they'd first met, she sat up impatiently. "Lust," she repeated stubbornly and reached for the bottle of sunscreen sitting on the table. "It was nothing but lust."

"How can you say that?" Megan cried. "You were crazy about him!"

Frowning, Rena smeared the cream over her legs. "*Crazy* being the operative word."

"Uggh," Megan groaned, obviously frustrated by having her words twisted around. "You weren't crazy! In fact, accepting Clayton's invitation to dance was probably the sanest and bravest thing you'd ever done in your life."

When Rena humphed her disagreement, Megan swung her legs over the side of the chair and snatched the bottle of sunscreen from Rena's hand. "You listen to me, Rena Rankin," she ordered sternly. "Up until that night, you'd lived your entire life at your parents' direction, being the dutiful daughter, the perfect little debutante, doing exactly what you were told, never daring to veer either left or right from the path they'd mapped out for you. But with Clayton you forgot all that, and you were simply *you!*"

"Me?" Rena sputtered a laugh. "I was twenty-one years old, extremely naive and looking for trouble. And I found it," she added bitterly.

"You *weren't* looking for trouble."

"Wasn't I?" Rena asked, arching a brow above the rim of her sunglasses as she peered at her friend. "Slumming. Isn't that what you called it that night when you suggested that the three of us go inside that country-western dance hall in Oklahoma City? Three sorority girls from the University of Oklahoma mixing and mingling with the local yokels, I believe is how you described it."

Megan's cheeks reddened, but she lifted her chin defensively. "Okay. So maybe my intentions weren't totally charitable, but I was proven wrong, wasn't I? The cowboys we met that night treated us with more respect than any of the fraternity boys ever had, didn't they?" She didn't wait for an answer. Didn't seem to want one. "They were gentlemen. Treated us like ladies. And we had fun, didn't we?"

"Yes," Rena agreed, with a decisive nod of her head. "We definitely had fun. But I paid for the fun I had that night."

Rena sighed heavily, weary from arguing with her friend. "Look, Megan," she said patiently, hoping to make her friend understand. "I know my leaving Clayton seems impulsive, irrational, maybe even a mistake. And perhaps it is,'' she admitted reluctantly. "But I've done a lot of thinking over the last few months. Not just about my relationship with Clayton, but about *me,* and I've discovered some things about myself that I don't like very much.

"For years I allowed my parents to control my life, based my happiness on their approval. And when I married Clayton, I simply transferred that control to him. I don't blame him,'' she said quickly when Megan appeared as if she was about to argue. "Not totally, anyway. Although I do believe things might have been different if Clayton had been willing to be more of a husband to me and more of a father to the children, if he'd only loved us more and been willing to show his love for us. But I realized that nothing was going to change for us or *me,*'' she added emphatically, "unless I made some changes myself.''

"And leaving Clayton is your answer to your problems?'' Megan asked doubtfully.

"Partially. I need to learn to stand on my own two feet. To be independent.'' Rena smiled softly, thinking of the steps she'd already taken in that direction. "I've bought a house in Salado, a wonderful old place that the twins and I can live in while I restore it. And I'm starting an interior design business, something I've always dreamed of doing but…'' she smiled ruefully, not wanting to place blame. "Well, let's just say I allowed others to keep me from pursuing that dream.''

"Oh, Rena,'' Megan began sorrowfully.

But before she could say more a shrill voice called from the patio. "Rena! Rena, dear! You have a guest.''

Hearing the displeasure in her mother's voice, Rena didn't need to turn to see who her visitor was…but she did, anyway. And when she did, she saw that Clayton was already walking down the flag-stone path that led to the pool, not waiting for an invitation to join her. His stride was long and loose, yet purposeful, his shoulders broad beneath a crisp black Western shirt. The jeans he wore hugged his hips and thighs and hung low over his boot heels, the starched denim fabric creating a soft whisking sound with each step he took on the uneven stone path.

Heat flooded her face at the sight of him, every nerve burning with awareness, and she was grateful that the sunglasses hid her eyes from him…without them she was certain he'd see the yearning in them.

"In fact, I'm still paying for that fun," she murmured under her breath.

Megan rose, smiling. "Clayton!" she called, her pleasure obvious. "It's so good to see you again."

Clayton swept off his hat and stretched out a hand, his expression guarded. "Megan. It's been a while."

"More than a while. Years!" she exclaimed, laughing as she squeezed his hand between hers. "How are you?"

Clayton glanced quickly at Rena, one corner of his mouth dipping into a scowl. "I've been better."

Megan glanced over her shoulder at Rena. "Yes," she said sympathetically as she turned back to Clayton. "I would imagine you have." She gave his hand a reassuring squeeze and rose to her toes to press a quick kiss to his cheek. "But the war's not over, yet," she whispered close to his ear.

She laughed when he ducked his head, his cheeks

reddening. "Still the same shy cowboy, I see," she teased.

"Clayton shy?" Rena snorted and rose from her chair. "That'll be the day."

"Sure he is," Megan replied and shot Clayton a sly wink. "And he's so cute when he blushes, don't you think?"

Rena glanced at Clayton, then away, frowning. "If you say so," she said, refusing to rise to the bait.

Clayton snugged his hat back over his head, irritated by his wife's indifference. "If you'll excuse us, Megan," he said, glaring at Rena's back. "Rena and I have some business to discuss."

"Clayton!" Rena cried in dismay, whirling to look at him. "How rude. Megan only just arrived."

"That's okay," Megan said, and scooped her purse from the patio table. "I need to go, anyway. I'm supposed to meet Harold at the club for lunch." She gave Rena a quick hug. "I'll call you later," she said, giving Rena a meaningful look, then turned to leave, whispering to Clayton as she brushed past him, "Hang in there, cowboy. I'm on your side."

Clayton waited until Megan was out of earshot before turning to Rena. "Where are the kids?"

Furious with him for the way he'd rushed Megan off, Rena dropped down onto the lounge chair and snatched up the bottle of sunscreen again. "With Dad."

"I'd like to see them."

"When?"

"Do I have to make an appointment to see my own kids?"

She heard the resentment in his voice and bit back her own caustic retort, knowing she wasn't being fair. After all, they were his children, too. "No," she replied as she spread the cream over her right calf. "But, in the future, you might want to call first to make certain they're here before you drop by."

Clayton watched her smooth the cream over her calf, then up her thigh, his gaze lingering on the sun-warmed flesh her skimpy bikini left exposed. Setting his jaw against the desire he felt rising, he dropped down on the foot of the chair Megan had vacated and braced his elbows on his thighs as he looked out across the pool. "When are we going to talk about this, Rena?"

"Talk about what?" she asked and calmly squirted more cream onto her palm.

He angled his head over his shoulder to look at her. "About our marriage."

She snorted a laugh and swept her hand across her middle, smearing the cream over her bare abdomen. "What marriage?"

"*Our* marriage," he shot back. "The one you seem so anxious to end."

"We don't have a marriage, Clayton. We have nothing but a legal document that binds us together."

"We damn sure do have a marriage, and a family, too," he told her furiously. "And I think it's high time you quit playing whatever little game this is you're playing and come home where you belong."

She slammed the bottle down on the table hard enough to make the carved iron legs wobble. Grabbing the chair's arms, she jerked herself forward and leaned across the distance that separated them, putting her face only inches from his. "This isn't a game, Clayton," she warned him darkly. "This is my life we're talking about."

He ripped off his hat, tossing it to the tiled deck that skirted the kidney-shaped pool, and twisted around to face her fully. Though frightened by the anger that turned his blue eyes to steel, Rena refused to shrink away from him.

"And mine," he grated out. "And, by God, I have a right to know why you left me."

"Why?" she asked, unable to keep the bitterness from her voice. "Does it hurt your male pride to have to tell your traveling buddies, Pete and Troy, that your wife left you?"

He reached out and grabbed her by the shoulders, taking her by surprise, and yanked her closer still, his fingers digging into her bare skin.

She struggled, trying to get free. "Clayton! Let go of me!"

He dug his fingers deeper. "Don't mess with me, Rena," he warned. "I've already listened to about all the verbal abuse I can stomach for one day."

She stilled immediately, her face going pale. "Mother," she whispered. "What did she say to you?"

He dropped his hands and twisted back around, bracing his forearms on his thighs again and scowling at the pool's shimmering surface. "Nothing."

She grabbed his elbow and tugged, but only succeeded in drawing herself to the edge of her chair, not turning him back to face her as she'd wanted. "Clayton!" she cried in frustration. "What did she say to you?"

He thinned his lips and narrowed his eyes. "Nothing that she hasn't said before." He gave his arm a jerk, pulling his elbow from her grasp. "I want to see my kids. When will they be back?"

"Soon," she murmured, staring at his stiff spine. "Dad wanted to take them to the office so he could show them off."

Clayton stood abruptly and crossed to the edge of the pool, bending to scoop his hat from the tile surface. With his back to her, he settled it over his head and ran his index finger along the edge of the brim in front, snugging it down low over his forehead. "I'm staying at the Wayfarer Inn on Interstate 40. Call me when they get back."

Rena watched him stride angrily back up the flagstone path toward the house. When he reached the patio, he hesitated a moment, then spun to the left and headed for the side yard and the gate that led to the driveway, obviously anxious to avoid another confrontation with her mother.

Two

Rena stood before the kitchen window, her arms hugged beneath her breasts, staring out at the pool and the lounge chair where Clayton had sat only moments ago. Though her skin still held the warmth of the sun, she rubbed her hands slowly up and down her arms, trying to ease the chill that penetrated to the bone. She could still see the hard set of Clayton's jaw, the stiffness of his spine, and knew that whatever her mother had said to him had hurt him deeply.

But that was nothing new, she thought wearily. Her mother had always delighted in making Clayton feel inferior—though Rena sometimes wondered who her mother hurt more with her biting comments...Clayton or Rena?

Nothing but a shiftless cowboy.

Married out of your class.

A man with his intellect and upbringing couldn't

possibly understand the needs and expectations of a woman with your background and breeding.

Rena had heard her mother's opinions of her marriage spouted throughout the four-plus years of her marriage to Clayton, but never delivered more smugly than when Rena had arrived in Tulsa with her children in tow and informed her parents that she had left Clayton.

No, her mother had never approved of Clayton, and Rena was sure that Gloria Palmer would feel no compunction at all in letting her son-in-law know exactly how she felt about him. Especially now, when she knew of Rena's plans to divorce him.

"Oh, there you are, dear."

Rena glanced over her shoulder as her mother swept into the kitchen, her expression a picture of innocence. "I didn't realize that I was lost," she said, trying, but failing, to keep from her voice the resentment her mother's appearance drew.

"And what has put you in such a foul mood?" her mother asked. "Or should I ask *who?*" she amended pointedly.

"What did you say to Clayton, Mother?"

"Say?" her mother repeated innocently. "Why nothing out of the ordinary."

No, Rena thought bitterly, it wouldn't be out of the ordinary for her mother to say something unkind to Clayton. But she knew that discussing it further would be a waste of her time. "Why were you looking for me?" she asked instead.

"To tell you that I made a few appointments for you." Her mother frowned as she took in Rena's current dress...or lack thereof. "But you'll need to hurry and change out of your swimsuit and into something more appropriate in order to make them on time.''

''What appointments?''

''At the day spa,'' her mother replied, looking pleased with herself. ''I thought you might enjoy an afternoon of pampering. Manicure, pedicure, a massage. And darling Jon Mark agreed to work you in for a shampoo and style, as well.''

Rena drew in a deep breath, fighting for patience. Forty-eight hours in her parents' home and her mother was already trying to take control of her life again. ''Thanks, Mother,'' she said as she brushed past her, ''but I already have plans for the afternoon.''

Gloria spun to stare after her. ''But the appointments have already been made! I simply *can't* cancel now. Not after Cecille went to such trouble to rearrange everyone's schedule, in order to work you in.''

Rena stopped and slowly turned. ''I'm sorry that Cecille will be inconvenienced. But, as I said, I have plans.''

Gloria planted her hands on her hips. ''And what plans could you have possibly made that are so important that they can't be changed?''

''I'm taking the twins to see Clayton this afternoon.''

Her mother stared at her a moment, then waved away Rena's plans as if unimportant. ''Well, if that's all that's keeping you from enjoying a day at the spa, then there's no problem. *I* can take the children to see Clayton.''

''That won't be necessary. I—''

Her mother held up a hand. ''I refuse to listen to another word. You're *going* to the spa.'' When Rena opened her mouth to argue further, her mother caught her hands in hers and squeezed, her expression turning solicitous. "Please, darling," she begged softly. "Let me do this for you. You've been under such a tremendous strain. An afternoon at the spa will do you a world of good. You'll see. Please say you'll go."

Rena felt herself weakening.

"Please?" her mother coaxed. "If not for yourself, then do it for me."

Knowing how fruitless it was to argue with her mother, Rena sagged in defeat. "Oh, all right. If you're sure you don't mind taking the children to see Clayton."

"Of course I don't mind, darling!" Gloria slipped an arm around Rena's waist and hugged her against her side. "And I don't want you worrying about a thing while you're at the spa," she lectured as she guided Rena to the rear staircase. "You just concentrate on enjoying yourself. No one deserves an afternoon of pampering more than you. Stuck out on that godforsaken ranch all alone with two young, active children." She made a tsking sound with her tongue. "I wonder how you stood it as long as you did."

After spending four hours at the day spa being pampered, polished and fawned over, Rena returned to her parents' home feeling relaxed and renewed. Maybe Mother was right, she reflected grudgingly as she entered the side door that opened from the portico into the kitchen. An afternoon of pampering might have been exactly what she needed to put her in a better frame of mind.

As she stepped into the kitchen, Brittany turned

from the breakfast bar, wearing a milk mustache. "Mommy!" she squealed, and flung her arms wide, inviting a hug.

"Hi, sweethearts," Rena said, catching both her children in an exuberant hug.

"Mrs. Carson made us cookies," Brandon said, his expression serious as always as he held up one, minus a bite, as proof.

Rena smiled fondly at the housekeeper who stood on the opposite side of the bar. "Spoiling them, I see."

Tipping up her nose, Mrs. Carson folded her hands primly at her waist. "No more than I did you, when you still lived at home."

Laughing because she knew what the housekeeper said was true, Rena plucked a chocolate chip cookie from the plate and took a bite before glancing down at the twins. "So what all did you two do this afternoon?"

"Went shopping with Nonnie."

Rena's smile slowly melted as she stared at Brittany. "Shopping? But didn't Nonnie take you to see Daddy?"

"Uh-uh. She took us to the mall. I got a new dress and a necklace, and Brandon got a watch."

"See?" Brandon said proudly, waving his arm in front of his mother's face.

Rena caught his wrist and pushed his arm back in order to admire the new watch. "Yes, I see," she said, forcing a smile for her son's sake.

She glanced over at Mrs. Carson. "And where is *Mother?*" she asked pointedly.

Avoiding Rena's gaze, the housekeeper set the plate of cookies on the counter in front of the twins and turned away. "Getting dressed for dinner," she said, then cast an uneasy glance over her shoulder and added, "She's invited a guest."

"Who?" Rena asked, praying that her mother had fulfilled her promise by inviting Clayton to dinner.

"Uncle Bill," Brittany supplied helpfully. "He's nice. When we were at Pawpaw's bank, he let me and Brandon play with his computer."

Furious with her mother for not taking the children to see Clayton as she'd assured Rena she would, Rena reached for the phone. "Set another plate, Mrs. Carson. We'll be having another guest for dinner."

The call Clayton had waited on all afternoon finally came while he was at the boarding facility, feeding and exercising his horse. But the message Rena had left for him with the hotel's switchboard operator, inviting him to join the Palmers for dinner, wasn't the one he'd expected, nor was it how he'd have chosen to spend his evening, if he'd been given a choice.

But he would have dinner at his in-laws' house, he told himself as he settled his hat over his head, if that's what it took to get to see his wife and kids.

Yet, even knowing he had an evening with his family to look forward to, Clayton still found himself stopping at the foot of the circular drive that curved in front of his in-laws' home and looking up at the stately mansion, feeling all the old inadequacies stealing over him.

Rena's childhood home had always intimidated him, as did her parents. The house screamed money and permanence, two things that had been conspicuously missing from his own life, until a few short years ago. And though he was sure his current net worth didn't come close to matching that of his wife's parents, he'd come a long way in closing the gap that had once separated them.

He'd worked hard at rodeoing and had made quite a name for himself, winning four World Champion Calf Roper buckles, and missing out on two other buckles by fractions of a second. With success had come commercial offers for endorsements, though he still couldn't get used to seeing his face plastered on billboards and staring back at him from glossy magazine ads.

And he'd thought he had created a sense of permanency, as well. The fifteen-hundred-acre ranch near Austin, Texas, was home to him…or at least it had been, before Rena had packed up the kids and left. Now the very thought of returning there alone made his stomach knot in dread.

He wouldn't go home alone, he told himself, and forced himself to take that first step up the drive. Rena, Brittany and Brandon would be going home with him. He wouldn't allow himself to even consider any other possibility.

Frowning, he punched the doorbell, then stepped back, listening to the muffled Westminster chime echo through the house's expansive interior. From the opposite side of the door, he heard the impatient click of high heels on the marble entry and knew who would greet him at the door. Tensing, he braced himself for the confrontation as the door opened.

"Good evening, Clayton." Mrs. Palmer offered him a stiff smile as she opened the door wider, inviting him in. "Everyone's in the solarium, enjoying the sunset. Why don't you join them while I check on dinner?''

Solarium? The word sounded as pompous and uninviting to Clayton as the woman who'd uttered it. Left to find his way to the room alone, he pulled off his hat with a sigh of resignation and tossed it onto the heavily carved marble table centered beneath the entry hall's dome-shaped ceiling, wishing he were most anywhere but there.

But then he heard the irresistible trill of Brittany's excited chatter, and he headed for the solarium. He caught sight of his daughter immediately, leaning over the side of the fountain, her stomach pressed flat against the smooth stone. Her arm was stretched out as far as she could reach, as she tossed pennies toward the base of the mermaid who rose from the fountain as if breaking through the ocean's surface.

"Whoa, shortcake," he said, and caught her by the hem of her dress, saving her from pitching face first into the fountain's pool. "You're supposed to toss the pennies, not personally deliver them."

Laughing, Brittany spun around and made a wild leap from the side of the fountain and straight into her daddy's arms, taking him by surprise.

"Daddy!" she cried, wrapping her arms around his neck and clinging. "You came!"

Stunned by the unexpected exuberance in her welcome, Clayton had to swallow back emotion at the feel of the little arms wound tightly around his neck. "Course, I did, shortcake." He gave her an awkward hug, then shifted her to his hip. "I was invited, wasn't I?"

Brittany put a hand at the side of her mouth and

leaned to whisper in his ear, "Yeah, but Nonnie said you wouldn't come."

Clayton turned to frown at the doorway just as his mother-in-law entered the solarium. "She did, did she?" he muttered, his frown deepening.

"Yeah. She said you didn't have the graces to eat with us, but I told her you did."

Clayton cocked his head to peer at his daughter in confusion. "Graces?" he repeated, frowning. Then slowly he realized what his mother-in-law must have said. "You mean social graces, don't you, short-cake?" he asked wryly.

"Yeah," she said, bobbing her head. "Social graces. Nonnie said you didn't have any, but you do, don't you, Daddy?"

Though he was tempted to leave right then and there, Clayton knew he wouldn't. Not and let his in-laws think they could run him off that easily. "Do you know what social graces are?" he asked her.

She pushed her lips out into a pout. "No. I asked Mommy, but she just kept yellin' at Nonnie and wouldn't answer me."

Clayton's eyebrows shot up. "Your mother was yelling at Nonnie?"

Brittany nodded her head again, making her pig-tails bob. "Uh-huh." Scrunching her nose up imp-ishly, she placed a hand at the side of her mouth again and leaned close. "And Mommy said a no-no word, too," she whispered, then clapped her fingers over her mouth to smother a giggle.

Though he would love nothing better than to ask his daughter why her mother was yelling at Nonnie, Clayton knew that wouldn't be right. Instead, he glanced around, looking for Rena. "Where is your mother?" he asked.

Brittany lifted a hand, pointing. "Over there."

At that moment Clayton saw his wife, stepping around a tall potted palm, smiling at something a man following her was saying. She froze when her gaze met Clayton's, and he would swear it was guilt he saw in her eyes before she looked away.

The jealous rage that swelled inside him was wild and dark, and tore through him like a wild bronc trying to bust his way out of a chute.

"Daddy," Brittany complained, wriggling in his arms. "You're hurtin' me."

Clayton immediately loosened his grip, unaware that, in his rage, he'd tightened his arms around her. "Sorry, shortcake," he murmured, unable to take his eyes off his wife. "Who's the man with Mommy?" he asked with a jerk of his chin in the direction of the two.

Brittany twisted around in his arms and looked. "Uncle Bill. He's nice," she said, turning to smile at Clayton. "He works at Pawpaw's bank."

A man from Pawpaw's bank, huh? So that's the plan, Clayton thought bitterly, as the pieces of the puzzle slowly clicked into place. Seemed Rena's parents were already busy picking out his replacement.

"Did I hear correctly?" Bill asked, smiling—or was that leering?—at Clayton over a glass of Bordeaux from the opposite side of the table. "You rope calves for a living?"

Clayton ground his teeth, but managed a civil tone when he replied, "Yeah, you heard correctly."

"And you get paid to do this?"

"When I win. But rodeoing isn't my sole source of income."

"Really?" Bill braced his elbows on the table and lazily swirled his wine around the bowl of the crystal goblet he held between hands that looked as pampered as any lady's. "And what other businesses are you involved in?"

"I endorse a line of Western wear and a line of roping supplies, plus we run around two hundred head of cattle on our ranch." He turned to Rena and forced a tight smile. "Don't we, dear?" he asked, emphasizing the "we" so that Bill would get the message that his wife was still very much married and off-limits.

"Yes," she said, and offered him a brittle smile in return. "We certainly do."

"Run cattle," Bill repeated thoughtfully as he sipped at his wine. "And what exactly does a man do when he 'runs' cattle?"

Clayton tried hard not to laugh. The man was more of a greenhorn than he'd first thought. "He raises them," he replied dryly. "We have a cow-calf operation, which means we keep a herd of mama cows on the ranch, and several bulls to service them. Come fall, we'll castrate most of the bull calves that were born last spring, then—"

He heard a silver fork clatter against bone china and glanced over to find Mrs. Palmer staring at him, her face mottled with indignation.

"Really, Clayton," she chided. "I hardly think this is appropriate dinner conversation."

Clayton gestured with his fork across the table at Bill. "He asked."

Her frown of disapproval deepened before she

turned it into an adoring smile as she shifted her gaze
to Bill. "I'm sure Bill was just being polite by in-
quiring about your business interests. Bill's quite a
successful man himself, you know. Not only has he
done a fine job heading up the trust department at
Martin's bank, he has also amassed a sizable fortune
for himself with his own investments."

Bill lifted his glass in a silent toast to Rena's father. "I had an excellent teacher."

"And he's built an elegant home on Grand Lake,"
Gloria added, "with the most stunning views. And
he designed it himself. He's quite talented, you
know. You must see it, Rena," she said, turning to
her daughter. "Perhaps you can persuade Bill to give
you a personal tour."

Abruptly, Rena shoved back her chair, her arm
striking Clayton's as she rose. He glanced up and
was surprised to see that her face was flushed with
anger.

"If you'll excuse me," she said tersely, then spun
and all but ran from the room.

Rena stood before the vanity in her bathroom, her
fingers curled tightly around the cold marble, forcing
herself to take long, deep, calming breaths. It didn't
help. Rage, white-hot and blinding, continued to burn
through her.

She felt as if she were caught in a game of human
tug-of-war. Her parents on one side; Clayton on the
other. Her trapped in the middle, being pulled first
one way, then the other, until she was sure she would
snap in two at the pressure being placed on her.

She whirled away from the vanity, scraping her
bangs from her forehead and holding them against

the top of her head. Coming to her parents, when she'd left Clayton, had been a mistake. She could see that now. But she'd wanted so badly for the twins to spend time with their grandparents, to get to know them better, and she'd thought that this would be the perfect opportunity.

With a moan of frustration, she dropped her arms, fisting her hands at her sides. But she should have known that once her parents knew of her plans to divorce Clayton, they would try to take control of her life again. The signs had all been there for her to see. Her father's offer to handle the legal proceedings of the divorce for her, the expensive gifts her parents plied the children with, the day at the spa arranged by her mother...

But her parents inviting Bill home for dinner had been the last straw. All but parading Bill beneath her nose, expounding on his accomplishments. Pushing. Pushing. Pushing. And in front of Clayton, no less.

She wouldn't fall into the trap they were placing carefully around her, she told herself. She had lived the first twenty-one years of her life under their manipulative thumbs, being the dutiful daughter, following the path they had carefully and strategically laid out for her.

But she wouldn't do so again.

Three more days, she reminded herself, inhaling deeply, searching for the strength she knew she would need to stand firm against them. Three more days, then she was leaving her parents' home and heading back to Texas and the new life she'd planned for herself there.

Three

———

With dawn less than an hour away and his in-laws' estate still draped in darkness, Clayton stole across the rear lawn, keeping to the shadows and avoiding the bright patches of moonlight scattered about. Grateful that his in-laws didn't have any dogs to alert them of his approach, he reached the portico that arched between the Palmers' four-car garage and their home, and paused to study the stone column support nearest him, wondering if he could pull this off.

Knowing that a desperate situation required desperate measures, he toed off his boots and tossed his hat on top of them. With a resigned sigh, he planted a foot against an uneven stone and hauled himself up. He stretched one arm up high, found a grip along the edge of the roof, then reached up with the other and, straining, hauled himself up. With the slate tiles

digging into his stomach, he hitched himself higher
and lifted a knee to brace against the roof's edge.
Breathing heavily, he heaved himself up, then stood,
dusting off his clothes as he looked around.

He studied the dark house a moment, slowly
counting the windows on the second floor, until he
found Rena's. Praying that his wife had left the window open an inch or two as was her habit at the
ranch, he crossed to where the portico's roof joined
with that of the main structure and half walked, half
crawled his way up the slight incline.

When he found the window open as he'd hoped,
he dug his pocketknife from his pocket, slipped the
blade between the screen and the window frame and
twisted until he'd worked the screen from the brack-
ets that held it in place. After setting the screen aside,
he eased the window up higher, swung a leg over
the sill and ducked inside the bedroom.

He stood a moment, letting his eyes adapt to the
change in light, before tiptoeing to the side of the
bed. His heart squeezed a bit as he gazed down at
his sleeping wife. Bathed in moonlight that spilled
through the open window behind him, she lay on her
side, one hand tucked between her cheek and her
pillow.

With his gaze on her sleeping profile, he lifted a
foot and dragged off first one sock, then the other.
Tossing them aside, he unbuckled his belt, and
quickly stripped off his jeans. As he eased closer to
the side of the bed, he caught his shirt's lowest button, releasing each disk in turn, until his shirt hung
open. Shrugging it off, he dropped it to the pile of
clothes already littering the floor, then lifted the corner of the sheet and slipped beneath the covers.

Stretching out beside his wife, he propped himself up on an elbow, content, for the moment, just to watch her sleep. When the urge to touch her became too strong, he lifted a hand and stroked the tips of his fingers beneath her eyelashes, then down along her jaw.

At his fingers' soft trailing, she snuggled deeper into her pillow, her lips parting on a thready sigh. The pleasure-filled sound hummed through Clayton, calling to something deep in his soul, and, unable to resist any longer, he lowered his face over hers. With a tenderness intended to seduce, he swept his tongue across her lower lip, then pressed his mouth lightly against the moisture he'd left there, warming her lips with his breath, before he began to slowly sip at the sweetness beyond.

He felt another sigh vibrate against his lips, and grew still when she shifted and drew her hand languidly from beneath her cheek to loop it loosely around his neck.

From experience, Clayton knew that her response to him was unconscious, instinctive. He knew, too, that what he was doing probably wasn't ethical, maybe not even legal...but for sure not fair. But at this point he wasn't concerned about playing by any set of rules, established or not. He needed to somehow break through Rena's resistance, reestablish their relationship, remind her of what they'd once shared.

And the bedroom was the one place they'd never had a problem communicating.

The idea to seduce his wife had come to him while he'd been lying in his bed at the motel, alone, miserable. Scared spitless that he was going to lose his wife and family, and frustrated because he hadn't been able to get Rena alone long enough to talk to her while at his in-laws' for dinner, he had come up with this plan.

He didn't doubt for a minute that he could pull off the seduction. A hundred or more times over the years, after arriving home in the middle of the night from a rodeo, he'd slipped into bed with Rena, without ever once waking her. At least not immediately. But eventually he would get around to drawing her from sleep with a slow seduction, much like the one he had planned for tonight.

Hoping that by catching her off guard, her mind dulled with sleep, she would respond naturally, even welcome him into her arms as she had so many times in the past, he let his hand slide down the smooth column of her throat. Feeling the thrum of her pulse beneath his palm, he marveled at it a moment, before he dropped his hand to a breast. He stroked a thumb over her nipple, bringing it to life beneath her nightgown's thin fabric, then smoothed his palm farther down her front and to her knees, where the hem of her nightgown was bunched. Pleased to at last meet bare skin, he closed his fingers around a shapely calf and squeezed.

She mewled at the gentle pressure, and he froze, holding his breath, as she shifted closer to him and molded her body against his. With her eyes still closed, her mind still obviously clouded with sleep, she lifted her head in a blind search for his mouth. Finding it, she purred her pleasure as she curled her fingers around his neck and drew him down with her. His body responded immediately to her lips' teasing, his already stiffening sex pushing against the gentle curve of her pelvis.

"Rena?" he whispered.

She hummed a sleepy response against his lips, then opened her mouth to mate her tongue with his in a slow, sensual dance.

Desire stabbed through Clayton and he fought it back, determined to keep his hands gentle, his need for her under control. Slowly, carefully, he eased her to her back, certain, by her response to him, that she wouldn't send him packing when she woke fully and found him in her bed. "Rena," he said again, more urgent this time.

She blinked open her eyes and slowly brought his face into focus. "Clayton?" she murmured in confusion, her voice still rough with sleep. Frowning slightly, she tried to sit up.

He pressed his mouth against hers, forcing her head back to the pillow. "Yeah, baby, it's me," he murmured. He felt the tension move through her, worried over it, then her breath whispered against his lips on a soft sigh of acceptance, and he knew his plan had worked.

He returned his hand to her calf and dragged his knuckles slowly up her leg, easing her nightgown higher. "It's been a long time, Rena," he whispered huskily. "A damn long time." When his hand reached the juncture of her thighs, her body convulsed instinctively and he groaned, cupping his hand over her sex as he drew back to meet her gaze. "Make love with me, Rena," he said softly, increasing the pressure.

Rena stared up at Clayton, fully awake now, her blood flowing like liquid fire through her veins. She saw the need in his eyes, the same need she knew must be mirrored in her own...and wondered if she could be dreaming. Needing the reassurance that he wasn't a figment of her imagination, a star player in a lustful dream, she laid a palm against his cheek. And nearly wept when her palm met the warmth of his flesh.

He turned his face into her hand, capturing her fingers with his own, and pressed his lips against the center of her palm. "Let me love you," he whispered, turning his gaze to hers again. "Let me love you, Rena."

Tears filled her eyes as she stared at him, lost in the depths of his blue eyes, wondering what his presence meant, and more, how she should respond to the question that burned in his eyes.

Say, yes, her heart urged. *It has been a long time. Make love with him. You've missed him so desperately, needed him for such a very, very long time. You want this. Him. Tell him yes.*

But her mind screamed a different response, one she didn't want to hear. *No! He's stayed away too long! Leaving you with not even the assurance of his love to keep you warm through the long, lonely nights. He wants your body, not your heart. He's never yet in the four-plus years of your marriage ever told you that he loves you. Stop before it's too late, before he hurts you again. Stop!*

At her mind's warning she squeezed her eyes shut, the familiar ache she'd lived with for so many years returning to spread through her heart, slamming doors behind it until it had sealed off every chamber, silencing her heart's urgings.

She opened her eyes to meet his gaze, prepared to

tell him no, that it had been *too* long, and order him
from her bed. But as soon as her gaze met his and
she saw the warmth, the hope, the uncertainty there,
the doors of her heart flew open again, letting him
in. "Yes," whispered, gulping back tears. "Love
me, Clayton."

Hearing the tears that thickened her voice, Clayton
hesitated, wondering if, later, she would harbor any
regrets…but quickly decided it didn't matter. She'd
agreed to make love with him, and he'd be damned
if he would question her decision to do so. He
stripped off his boxers, flung them aside, then eased
down beside her and placed his hand on her leg
again. He held her gaze while he dragged his fingertips back up her thigh, then trailed them higher along
the folds of her sex, making her shiver.

"Cold?" he asked as he sifted his fingers through
soft feminine curls.

She nodded as she laid a hand against his face,
shaping her palm over his cheek. "A little."

He dipped his head, nudging the nightgown to her
waist with his nose, and pressed his lips against her
stomach to lave the skin with his tongue. "I'll warm
you up," he promised, even as he began to stroke a
fire to life between her legs.

She arched, moaning, and he withdrew to meet her
gaze. "I've missed you, Rena."

Tears budded at the huskiness in his voice and she
stroked her palm across his cheek. "And I've missed
you," she murmured, then gasped, stiffening when
he stroked a knuckle across her moist center.

"Did I hurt you?" he asked in concern.

She shook her head, her gaze riveted on his. "No.
I'm just…sensitive."

Not wanting to rush things, he drew his hand away and smoothed it over her abdomen. "Let's get rid of this," he suggested, pushing against the fabric bunched at her waist.

She nodded and sat up, gathering the nightgown within fingers that trembled, then tugged it up and over her head. She froze with her arms fully extended, the gown held high above her head, when she found Clayton had braced himself higher, his face now level with hers. The heat of his blue eyes burned into hers.

He took the gown from her and tossed it aside. "Better," he murmured and lowered his gaze to her breasts. "Much better," he added with a lusty sigh as he closed a hand over a breast and molded his palm around its firm shape. He dipped his head to lave the opposite breast, then drew back, smoothing a thumb over the moisture he'd left there. "So sweet," he whispered, then, unable to resist, leaned to draw the rosy center deeply into his mouth.

Lightning, white-hot and numbing, shot straight to Rena's center and burned. Weakened by it, by him, she filled her hands with his hair, holding him to her. Gulping at air, she let her head fall back and allowed the sensations to take her.

Tears burned behind her lids at the gentleness of his lovemaking, at the familiar tug of his greedy mouth on her breast. Oh, how she'd missed him, yearned for him, for this. Even as the thoughts formed, her center throbbed and turned molten with long-denied need.

"Clayton," she whispered, opening her eyes and forcing his mouth from her breast. When he looked up at her, the heat in his eyes seared through her, burning away all rational thought, and she simply stared.

"What?" he asked softly, bracing himself higher on his elbow to peer at her.

Feeling totally undone, helpless, she drew her hands to his cheeks, smoothing her thumbs along the high ridges of his cheekbones, trying to remember why she'd said his name. "I want to touch you," she murmured, and let her hands fall to his shoulders. "Just as you touched me," she whispered and dragged her palms to his chest. Pressing against the pads of muscle there, she rose to her knees and forced him down. Her gaze on her hands' movements, she smoothed them across his taut abdomen, sighing at the hard cords of muscle that rippled beneath her palms.

A low, lust-filled groan slipped past her lips as her gaze met his stiff arousal, rising from a nest of dark, coarse hair. Easing closer to his side, she gathered him in her hand and brushed a thumb over the swollen head of his sex. He flinched at the light caress, then moaned, and she glanced over, smiling as she stroked her fingers down his length. "Cold?" she teased.

"No," he said, and moaned again as she stroked her fingers back up. "In fact, I'm burning up."

She laughed softly, then dipped her head, pressing her lips low on his stomach.

When her tongue dipped into his navel and swirled, Clayton nearly lost it. Months of deprivation swelled, demanding an immediate and satisfying release. With a low growl, he caught her by her waist and lifted her over him, planting her knees firmly on either side of his hips. His gaze on hers, his heart pounding hard enough within his chest to crack a rib, he lifted his head to capture her mouth with his. "I want you, Rena," he murmured, nipping at her kiss-swollen lips. "I want all of you."

Even as he made his intentions known, she was guiding his sex to hers. He groaned at the first contact, closing his eyes against the heat, the honeyed moistness that greeted him, then raised his hips and pushed inside. He froze, clamping his hands down on her hips, holding her in place as her feminine walls closed around him, sure that if she moved so much as a muscle, he would lose what little control he'd managed to hold on to.

Wanting to make this last as long as possible, to touch her, love her in ways he knew would drive her wild, he dragged in a deep, fortifying breath, opened his eyes and eased her down inch by glorious inch. He kept his gaze on hers as he slowly filled her, watching as the passion rose to stain her cheeks, cloud her eyes. Distracted by a breast that bobbed into view, he lifted a hand to capture it and raked his thumb across her nipple…then watched the color on her cheeks deepen, her eyelids grow heavy and drift closed against the heat. In spite of his determination to make this last, his own body throbbed with need, demanding release.

He set the rhythm quickly, and she matched it, then set a faster one for him to follow, bracing her hands against his chest as she rode him with a wild abandon. Perspiration beaded his skin as he strained to hold back, to give her the pleasure she needed, deserved from him, before taking his own.

Surrounded by her sweetness, her heat, he set his jaw against the pleasure that knifed through him, and strained to pierce her farther still, wanting, needing to possess her fully, to restake his claim on his wife. Feeling the pressure build inside him, and knowing he couldn't last much longer, he thrust his hips high and buried himself to the hilt.

She arched hard against him and dropped her head back, sobbing out his name. Feeling the dig of her nails into his flesh, he sat up with a feral growl, locked an arm around her waist and held her against him, pushing her over the edge. He felt her shatter around him, found his own release and pumped his hot seed into her, feeling as if he were draining his very soul. He shuddered once…twice, clutching her to him…then sank back to the bed, bringing her with him, spent. With a shuddered sigh, he wrapped his arms around her and snuggled her against his chest. He held her to him, feeling the thunder of her heart against his, the stroke of her hand across his chest, and was sure that he had accomplished what he'd set out to accomplish. He pressed his lips against her hair. "Come home with me, Rena," he whispered. "Let's pack up the kids and head home."

Rena froze at his request, then slowly lifted her head to peer at him, the desire to say yes burning in her throat, in her heart. But she wouldn't agree to go home with him. Couldn't. Not until she knew things would be different for them this time. Not until he said the words she longed to hear.

"Why?" she asked, her voice trembling. "Tell me why you want me to come home with you, Clayton?"

He reared back to stare at her, then frowned and glanced away, avoiding her gaze. "Because you belong there," he said gruffly. "It's our home."

She stared at his profile, ice slowly spilling through her veins as she realized too late what she'd done. She'd welcomed him into her bed, exposed her heart. And he'd broken it all over again.

The moisture that filled her eyes spilled over her lashes as she rolled away from him. "No," she said, her voice thick with tears. "I'm not going home with you."

Stunned, Clayton pushed himself to an elbow, watching as she rose from the bed and stooped to pick up her nightgown from the floor.

"Why?" he asked as she headed for the adjoining bath. "You still want me. You can't deny that you do."

She stopped in the doorway and turned, one hand on the door, the other clutching the nightgown to her breasts, her heart breaking a little more. "No, I won't deny that I still want you," she said, tears streaming down her face. "But then, sex was never our problem, was it?" Her breath hitched painfully, and she closed the door between them, not wanting him to see how much he'd hurt her.

Clayton heard the lock turn, then lunged to his feet and charged for the door. He pounded a fist against it. "Rena! Open the door!" he shouted. "Don't lock me out. Talk to me. Please," he cried desperately, pressing his fist against the panel of wood, "just open the door and talk to me. We can work this out."

He lifted his fist to pound again, but whirled at the sound of another fist hitting the bedroom door across the room.

"Rena!" he heard her father yell from the other side of the locked door. "What's going on in there?

Are you all right? Do you want me to call the police?''

Clayton dropped his forehead against the bathroom door, feeling the frustration rising, the anger. The tears.

"Rena!" her father shouted again. "Is Clayton in there? Has he hurt you? I'm calling the police!"

Clayton slowly lifted his head to stare at the door Rena had closed between them and laid a palm against the unrelenting wood, as if to touch her. "I'm coming back," he whispered. "I'm coming back for you and the kids. And I'm taking you back home where you belong."

He heard his mother-in-law's shrill voice join with that of his father-in-law's, and knew his in-laws wouldn't hesitate to call the police. They'd do anything to get rid of him.

Hoping to spare Rena that last humiliation, he dragged the back of his hand across his eyes and grabbed his jeans from the floor. He jerked them on, then snatched up his shirt and socks. With a last wistful glance at the bathroom door, he turned for the window and the roof beyond.

"Hi, Daddy!"

At the sound of his daughter's cheerful voice, Clayton tightened his fingers around the receiver, his heart squeezing in his chest. "Mornin', shortcake. Put Mommy on the phone, okay?"

"She's still asleep."

Clayton frowned, glancing at his watch. "Well, would you wake her up for me? Tell her Daddy needs to talk to her."

"I— Wait, Nonnie!" Brittany cried. "I'm talking to my daddy."

There was a fumbling sound and Clayton could hear Brittany's muffled complaint before his mother-in-law's voice came across the line.

"What do you want, Clayton?" she asked crisply.

Clayton clenched his teeth. "I want to talk to my wife."

"She's resting and I refuse to wake her. She had a very emotional night," she added, the accusation in her tone letting Clayton know who she blamed for her daughter's current state of exhaustion.

"Then give her a message. Tell her that I've gone to a rodeo in South Dakota. But tell her I'm coming back at the end of the week."

"Yes, I'll tell her."

Before he could say more, there was a click and the line went dead. Clayton slammed down the receiver, swearing.

"That's it," he muttered darkly. As soon as he'd competed in the South Dakota rodeo, he was heading straight back to Oklahoma. And this time, he was taking Rena and the kids back to Texas. He wasn't going to allow his in-laws to interfere in his marriage any longer.

And he wasn't going to allow them to find Rena a replacement for him.

Rena sat opposite her mother at the breakfast table, hiding behind the morning newspaper, hoping that in doing so, she could thwart any attempt by her mother to broach the topic of Clayton's late-night visit to her parents' home.

"Imagine him breaking into our home in the middle of the night like some robber."

Gritting her teeth at her mother's superior tone, Rena gave the pages of the paper a firm snap, determined to ignore her.

"Sometimes, Rena, I wonder what possessed you to marry that man."

Rena shot her mother a quelling look, tipping her head discreetly toward the twins.

"Oh, for heaven's sake," her mother said, dismissing Rena's silent warning with a wave of her hand. "It isn't as if the children aren't aware of their father's shortcomings."

"Mother," Rena warned.

"What's shortcomings mean?" Brittany asked.

"Eat your cereal, Brittany," Rena ordered, then turned back to her mother. "I would appreciate it if you would refrain from making comments like that in front of my children."

"Comments like what? I merely said—"

"I *know* what you said, Mother. It isn't necessary to repeat it."

"Fine," Gloria said with an indignant sniff. "But I am entitled to my opinions, you know."

"Yes, but you don't need to air them in front of little ears."

"That's us," Brittany whispered to Brandon.

"Brittany!" Rena cried in frustration. "I told you to eat your cereal."

"Now look what you've done," her mother chided when tears swelled in Brittany's eyes. "You've made the poor dear cry." She rose from her chair and plucked Brittany from her booster. "There, there, snookums," she soothed, cradling the child's cheek against hers as she swayed back and forth. "You don't have to eat that nasty old cereal, if you don't want to."

"Yes, she does," Rena said furiously and stood, intending to return her daughter to her booster.

But Gloria turned away, preventing Rena from taking her granddaughter from her. "Not in Nonnie's house, she doesn't," she snapped, then puckered her lips and cooed to Brittany, "Nonnie knows what's best for her little girl, doesn't she, snookums?"

"That's it," Rena muttered angrily and threw her napkin down on the table. "We're leaving."

Gloria spun, her mouth dropping open. "What? But you said you were staying until Sunday! You can't leave now!"

"Oh, yes, I can," Rena told her. "You can't tell me what to do anymore, Mother. I'm not a child."

"As if you ever listened to me even then," her mother returned spitefully. "If you had, you wouldn't have married Clayton in the first place. You would have married someone more suitable, someone of your own class. Someone like Bill. Not that shiftless cowboy who hasn't the intelligence or the ambition to do anything but rope calves. With a little encouragement from you, you could have Bill. I know you could. And he would make a much better husband for you and father for these children."

Brittany lifted her head from her grandmother's shoulder to peer tearfully at her mother. "I don't want Bill to be my daddy," she sobbed pitifully. "I want my real daddy."

Shaking with anger, Rena snatched Brittany from her mother's arms and shifted her to her hip. "Don't worry, sweetheart," she told her daughter as she leaned to scoop a wide-eyed Brandon from his booster and onto her opposite hip. "Your daddy will always be your daddy, no matter what."

Her hands still trembling with rage, Rena dialed the number of the motel where Clayton was staying, then tucked the receiver between shoulder and ear and continued to pack.

"Wayfarer Inn. How may I direct your call?"

"Clayton Rankin, please," Rena requested as she scooped her toiletries from the vanity and into her makeup bag.

"I'm sorry," the operator said after a moment. "Mr. Rankin has already checked out."

The makeup bag slipped from Rena's fingers. "Checked out?" she asked in surprise. "Are you certain?"

"Yes. He checked out early this morning."

Suddenly feeling weak, Rena sank to her knees. "Did...did he leave any messages?"

"No, I'm sorry. Is there anything else I can help you with?"

Rena shook her head. "No," she said slowly. "But thank you."

She gulped back a sob as she pressed the button to disconnect.

Clayton had left without even saying goodbye.

Sniffling, she stooped to rake the spilled toiletries back into her bag. The tears pushed harder against her throat when she saw the packet of birth control pills lying on the floor. Picking it up, she sank back on her heels, remembering the previous night of passion with Clayton.

She sniffled again and shoved the packet deep into her makeup bag.

Well, at least this time she wouldn't have to worry about getting pregnant, she reflected miserably.

But having Clayton's children was never the problem. Winning his love was.

Five days later, and several thousand dollars richer, Clayton returned to Tulsa, having firmed up his decision while he was away.

He was packing up his wife and kids and taking them home to their ranch in Texas.

He knew that Rena would pitch a fit when he told her to load up the kids, that he was taking them all home, but he didn't see any other way for them to resolve whatever problems she thought they had with their marriage unless they returned home and to neutral ground. He sure as hell hadn't been able to discover her grievances with him when he'd been in Tulsa before. But he suspected that part of the problem, if not all of it, was due to her parents' interference. They were so busy filling her mind with his inadequacies and parading possible replacements past her that he didn't stand a chance of talking to his wife, much less working out any problems with her. Not as long as she remained in Tulsa and within her parents' influence.

And he sure as hell wasn't going to sit quietly by and allow his in-laws to squeeze him right out of his family's lives. Not without first putting up one hell of a fight.

Approaching the Palmers' home, he started to pull his truck and horse trailer to the curb, knowing how much his mother-in-law detested him parking his vehicle on her driveway, then muttered, "To hell with her," and steered his truck onto the curved drive, coming to a stop directly opposite the front door.

After jumping down from his truck, he strode to the side of the trailer and to the open window where Easy's head appeared. "If you feel the call of nature," he murmured to his horse as he reached to scratch the animal between the ears, "dump a load out the window."

Chuckling at the image of Mrs. Palmer's face, if Easy were to manage to soil her pristine drive, he gave the horse a final pat and jogged for the door. After punching the doorbell, he shifted impatiently from one foot to the other, praying Rena would answer the door and not her mother.

But when the door opened, it was Mrs. Carson, the Palmers' housekeeper who appeared.

"Clayton!" she said in surprise. "What are you doing here?"

"I came to see Rena. Would you get her for me?"

Mrs. Carson glanced nervously over her shoulder, then stepped out onto the porch. "She's not here," she said in a low voice.

"Where is she?"

"Gone."

"Gone!" he repeated in surprise.

"Yes. She packed up the children several days ago and left."

Unaware that Rena had been planning on leaving her parents' home, Clayton could only stare.

"I gather that she and her parents had words," Mrs. Carson confided, nervously wringing her hands. "Mrs. Palmer has been in her room ever since, suffering from one of her migraines."

Clayton swore under his breath, angry with himself for letting his in-laws chase him off before he'd had a chance to finish his discussion with Rena. "Do you know where she was headed?"

Mrs. Carson caught her lower lip between her teeth and glanced over her shoulder again and into the house. She stared a moment, then squared her shoulders and turned back to face Clayton. "Salado. I saw the address on a piece of paper lying on Mr. Palmer's desk."

"Salado? Who does she know in Salado?"

"I'm not sure, but I remember the address. Box 19, Ranch Road 12."

Grateful for the information—information that he was sure would get Mrs. Carson fired if the Palmers ever found out she'd shared it with Clayton—he caught her hand in his and squeezed. "Thanks, Mrs. Carson."

Sniffing, the woman tipped up her chin. "A man has a right to know where his family is." She flapped a hand at him, shooing him away. "Go on," she urged. "Go after her. Rena needs you."

Praying that what the housekeeper said was true, impulsively Clayton dropped a kiss on her wrinkled cheek. "I hope so, Mrs. Carson. I sure hope so," he said again, then turned and loped down the steps.

Four

It took Clayton a little more than six hours to make the drive from Tulsa to Salado...six hours in which to work up a pretty good steam.

How the hell were he and Rena supposed to work out whatever problems she had with their marriage, he asked himself, if she kept running away every time he got near her or pressed her for answers?

"Making me chase her all the way to Oklahoma and back," he muttered angrily as he took the Salado exit off Interstate 35. "Locking herself in the bathroom and refusing to come out and talk to me? What the hell kind of game is she playing, anyway?"

Well, she could damn well dance him a slow waltz all the way across Texas, he told himself as he saw a sign indicating that Ranch Road 12 lay a quarter of a mile ahead, but he wasn't giving up. He'd chase her to hell and back, if that's what it took to save his marriage.

Unsure where he was going—or how he'd keep himself from strangling Rena when he arrived—he made the turn onto Ranch Road 12, scanning the numbers on the mailboxes as he drove down the two-lane country road.

He passed right by the mailbox with 19 hand-painted on its side before he could make out the weathered numbers, and had to reverse in order to make the turn onto the long, potholed drive lined by towering cedars.

Frowning at the old two-story house that came into view, he wondered if he'd read the address correctly. But then he saw Rena's Lincoln Navigator parked beneath a tree beside the house and knew that this had to be the right place. Parking his truck alongside his wife's SUV, he cut a glance toward the house, his frown deepening. A couple of sheets of tin were missing from the steep roof of the two-story stone structure, and the shutters that flanked the front windows hung at odd angles and flapped in a light afternoon breeze. What the hell was Rena doing in a place like this? he asked himself irritably. The house looked as if it had been abandoned for years!

Prepared to give his runaway wife a piece of his mind for leading him on this wild-goose chase across two states and back, he opened the door to his truck and jumped to the ground. Ramming his hat down firmly on his head, he headed for the front porch and the sagging screen door. He rapped twice, listening as he squinted to peer through the rusted screen, then called out, ''Rena!'' when he didn't hear a reply.

Still not hearing a response, he spun on his heel

and looked around, scowling, but saw no sign of life and heard no sound, other than the chirping of birds roosting high in the live oak trees that shaded the house.

Sure that his family had to be somewhere nearby, he crossed to the edge of the porch, braced a hand on the railing and vaulted over, then marched to the rear of the house. And that's where he found the twins, both with their backs to him and their heads shoved into the open doorway of a small shed.

He quickened his step and yelled, "Brittany! Brandon!"

They jumped, then turned, their eyes wide with surprise as they peered up at him.

"What are you kids doing?"

Brittany grinned up at him. "Hi, Daddy. We're watching Mommy work," she informed him in that matter-of-fact way of hers, then turned to poke her head inside the shed again.

Wondering what in the world Rena could be doing inside the shed, Clayton braced a hand against the weathered door frame and leaned to peer over his children's heads. What he saw made his jaw sag. If Brittany hadn't told him it was her mother inside the shed, he would never have recognized the woman kneeling on the hard-packed ground. Rena—his debutante, high-society wife, who always looked as if she'd just stepped off the page of some glossy fashion magazine cover—had a bandanna tied around her head and was wearing an old, stained shirt, her knees poking through the holes of a pair of threadbare jeans. He watched her fight with a wrench almost twice the size of her hand for a good ten seconds before he managed to find his voice. "Rena?"

She dragged a wrist across her damp forehead, leaving a streak of black grease behind, before turning to frown at him. "What are you doing here?" she muttered resentfully.

"What are *you* doing here?" he shot back.

"I live here."

"Since when?"

"Since five days ago, although I bought the place long before that." She tossed the wrench aside and rose to face him. "But don't worry. I didn't use your money to purchase the property. I used the inheritance Grandmother Palmer left to me."

Clayton curled the hand he held against the door frame into a fist. "I wasn't worried about how you paid for it," he growled. "But I *am* wondering why you felt the need to buy a house in Salado, when you already have a home not much more than a hour's drive from here."

She snatched a rag from the back pocket of her jeans and rubbed furiously at the grease that stained her hands. "The ranch isn't my home," she informed him coldly. "It's yours."

"Like hell it—" He glanced down to find the twins staring up at him, wide-eyed and hanging on his every word. Knowing that they didn't need to hear what all he had to say to their mother—or the words he might use—he dropped his hand to his side and jerked his chin toward the pump motor she'd been working on. "What's the problem with the well pump?"

"It quit working."

"And *you're* going to fix it?"

She planted a fist on her hip. "Do you see anyone else around to do the job?"

He returned her stony gaze with one of his own, then growled, "Yeah. Me," and brushed past the twins and stepped into the shed's shadowed interior.

Though he could see that Rena resented his back-handed offer of help, she stepped aside, making room for him in the small space. He circled the pump, examining it. "What happened?"

"I don't know," she said, dragging a frustrated hand through her hair. "It was working just fine, until about an hour ago."

"So you don't have any water in the house," he said, stating the obvious as he hunkered down for a closer look.

"Brilliant deduction, Clayton," she muttered dryly. "Just brilliant."

He glanced up at her, meeting her mulish gaze a long moment, before turning to look at the twins. "Can you kids reach the faucet at the kitchen sink?"

"Yeah," Brandon replied, swelling his chest proudly. "We got a step stool to stand on."

"Then run back up to the house and turn it on," Clayton instructed, "and give me a holler when water comes out."

The twins took off at a run, arguing with every step over which one of them got to carry out their daddy's instructions.

When they were out of hearing distance, Clayton braced a wide hand on his thigh and spun on his heel to glare up at Rena. "Why didn't you tell me you were planning on leaving Oklahoma?"

"Why didn't you tell me *you* were leaving?" she shot back.

"I left a message for you."

"You did not! I called your motel and specifically

asked if you'd left any messages and was told that you hadn't.''

"That's because I didn't leave the message at the motel. I left it with your—''

Rena groaned, pressing her hand against her forehead. "Mother," she finished for him, then dropped the hand with a weary sigh. "She didn't tell me.''

"Figures," Clayton muttered, then scowled, adding another grievance to the long list he'd already prepared against his in-laws. "How long have you been planning this, anyway?''

"Planning what?" she asked in confusion.

"On leaving me.''

She stared at him a moment, two spots of color rising to stain her cheeks, before she dropped her gaze. "I don't know," she mumbled, looking guilty as hell. "A while, I guess.''

"So why the hell didn't you ever say something to me about your plans?''

She snapped her head up to glare at him. "And when was I supposed to have said something? You were never home.''

He leaped to his feet and shoved his face close to hers. "That's a damn lie, and you know it. I've been home.''

She arched a brow, undaunted by his threatening stance. "Really? That's odd, because I don't remember seeing you there recently.''

He swore and spun away, then whirled back, leveling a finger at her nose. "I'm a professional cowboy. I travel the circuit. You knew that when you married me.''

She shoved his hand away from her face. "Yes, I

did. But what I didn't know was that you would put your career before your family."

"That's bull, Rena, and you know it!"

"Is it? When was the last time you were home, Clayton? Better yet, when was the last time you *called* home?"

He frantically racked his brain, trying to remember when he'd last called. When he couldn't, he spun, turning his back to her, hiding his own guilt. "I can't name dates," he mumbled.

"No, I doubt that you can. Your memory isn't that long. But then, neither is mine. It's been so long ago, I can't remember, either."

He drew in a long breath, fighting for calm as he turned to face her again, knowing that arguing with her wouldn't do him any good. Not when what she said was true. "Okay, so maybe I haven't been home in a while, or called as often as I should, but is that any reason to leave me?"

"That's not the only reason I left."

"Well, what are your reasons, then!" He swung an arm toward the open doorway, gesturing at the house beyond. "And what the hell are you trying to prove by buying this dump, when you've already got a perfectly nice house to live in?"

Rena stared at him, wondering how he could be so blind to her needs, to the problems that existed in their relationship, and knowing that trying to explain to him something that she was only beginning to understand herself was impossible. "You wouldn't understand," she said and turned away.

"Try me."

She swung back around to face him. "Because I

wanted a home!'' she cried. ''Something of my very own. Something that belonged just to me.''

He swore under his breath, then, unable to control his temper, shouted, ''Dammit! You *have* a home. With me!''

She took a step back toward the door. ''No. I don't have a home with you, Clayton,'' she said, her voice beginning to tremble. ''I never did.'' Turning, she ducked through the doorway, then ran to the house, leaving Clayton in the well house alone.

Clayton dipped his hands beneath the faucet and scrubbed at the grease that stained his hands, his butt all but dragging. The long drive from South Dakota back to Oklahoma, sleeping in his truck when exhaustion forced him from the road. The six-plus-hour drive from Tulsa to Salado. Another two hours sweating in the cramped shed, while he worked on the cantankerous pump. And for what?

''Don't have a home,'' he muttered under his breath as he hit the faucet handle with the back of his wrist, shutting off the water. He snatched up a dish towel from the worn countertop and dried his hands as he looked around the outdated kitchen. With its glass-fronted cabinets, scarred linoleum floor and ancient appliances, the room presented a sharp contrast to the modern, high-tech kitchen at their ranch…the house Rena insisted had never been her home.

Feeling the frustration building, he glanced up at the ceiling, hearing the creak of old wood overhead, and knew by the sound that Rena had finished putting the twins to bed and was on her way back downstairs. Tossing the dish towel aside, he headed for the hallway that led to the front of the house and the stairway that climbed to the second floor, ready to have it out with his wife, once and for all. He met her as she stepped from the last step and into the wide entry hall.

"We're finishing this discussion. Right here, right now."

She met his gaze stubbornly, letting a good five seconds hum by before she firmed her lips and brushed past him, headed for the front door. He followed, sensing that she didn't want the children to overhear whatever they might have to say to each other. But that was fine with him. He didn't think the kids needed to hear what they had to say to each other, either.

He let the screen door squeak closed behind him, watching as Rena stopped at the edge of the porch steps and hugged her arms beneath her breasts, her spine stiff.

Muttering a curse under his breath at her defensive stance, he crossed to stand beside her. With his gaze narrowed on the dark sky, he leaned forward, bracing his hands on the porch railing. "Why, Rena? Why are you doing all this?"

"Because I can't go on living with things the way they are."

He snapped his head around to look at her. "*What* things?" he cried in frustration.

She drew in a long, shuddery breath before turning her head to meet his gaze. "Us, Clayton. Us."

Seeing the tears in her eyes, hearing the tremble of them in her voice, and unable to respond to either, he whipped his head around to glare at the dark landscape. "And what exactly is wrong with *us?*"

She dropped her head back, groaning her frustration. "That *is* the problem. There is no 'us,' Clayton. We don't have a relationship. We never have. We simply share an address and a bed, when the mood strikes you."

He slammed a fist against the railing, making her flinch, then whirled to face her. "Dammit, Rena! Haven't I provided you with a home, seen that you and the kids have everything you need, everything you could possibly want? What the hell is it you expect from me?"

She stared at him, her eyes filling with tears, looking as if he'd just knocked the daylights out of her. "Nothing," she whispered, and turned for the door. "Absolutely nothing."

Clayton caught her by the arm, stopping her before she escaped. "Dammit, Rena!" he cried angrily, spinning her around to face him. "You're not running away again. You're going to stay right here until we settle this."

She snatched her arm from his grasp, her brown eyes dark with fury as she backed a step away from him. "Don't you dare think that you can tell me what I can and cannot do," she warned him furiously. "I've lived my entire life by someone else's rules. First my parents', then yours. Well, I'm not doing it any longer." She reached for the door again, jerked it open. "From now on, I'm living my life *my* way and by *my* rules. No one is ever going to have the power to control me again."

"Now wait just a damn minute," he said, and flattened a palm against the door, slamming it shut before she could escape him again. "I've never asked you to do anything, much less tried to control you or expect you to live by any set of rules.''

"Maybe not in so many words, but you stuck me out on that ranch and left me there, expecting me to stay.''

He tossed his hands up in the air. "Dammit, Rena! If you weren't happy living on the ranch, why didn't you say so? I thought you liked it there!''

"I *do* like the ranch,'' she cried, her frustration rising to equal his. "But I *don't* like living there alone.'' Tears filled her eyes, and she dug her fingers through her hair, trying to force them back. When she couldn't, she dropped her arms wearily to her sides and drew in a ragged breath as she met his gaze again. "I had dreams and plans for my life, Clayton, the same as you did for yours. But I put my dreams aside when we married and moved to the ranch, while you went right on chasing yours.''

Stunned as much by the tears that streamed down her face as he was by what she'd said, Clayton stared, speechless, unable to think of a thing to say in return. He'd robbed her of her dreams? What dreams? What the hell was she talking about?

Rena waited for a response from Clayton, some indication that he understood her unhappiness, her discontent, and was willing to discuss it. When none was forthcoming, she dragged the back of her hand across her cheek, then gave her chin a lift, clinging to her pride. "I want a divorce, Clayton. You can file, if you want, or I will. It doesn't matter. But we're getting a divorce.''

Something in Rena's voice—a certainty of purpose, a calmness despite the earlier storm—chilled Clayton to the bone. This wasn't a game she was playing, he realized slowly, his gaze riveted on her face. This wasn't some dramatic stunt she was pulling in order to get his attention. She really intended to go through with this. She was going to divorce him.

And something deep in his gut told him that there wasn't a damn thing he could do or say to change her mind.

When she reached for the door again, Clayton didn't try to stop her. He simply stood on the porch and watched her close the door between them, shutting him out of her life.

Memories from the past knifed through him at the sound of the door closing, and he squeezed his eyes shut against them, trying to block them out. But the images grew, filling his mind, tearing at his heart. A five-year-old little boy, standing on the curb, waiting for a bus, watching his uncle Frank walking away. The feeling of abandonment, the fear that had filled him.

He felt the tears rising, the grief tearing at his heart.

Then he heard Rena turn the lock. The sound echoed the breaking of his heart.

Rena stood at her bedroom window, a hand braced against its wooden frame, staring down through the darkness, watching as Clayton crossed the lawn to his truck.

Emotion rose to her throat, choking her, when she saw the dejected slump of his shoulders, the hands stuffed deep into the pockets of his jeans, and knew that she had hurt him. But she hadn't wanted to hurt him. Why would she want to hurt the only man she'd ever loved, the man she still loved with all of her heart?

She pressed a hand against her lips to hold back the sob that rose as she watched him climb into his truck and close the door behind him. As she listened to him rev the engine, she told herself again that she had done the right thing, knew that she'd had no other choice. It wasn't enough to know that Clayton wanted her with him, wanted her to remain as his wife. She wanted, needed, so much more from him.

She wanted and needed his love.

But how could she explain her needs to him, a man who thought that providing for her physical needs, showering her with material gifts, was enough? How could she make him, a man who seemed incapable of displaying affection outside the bedroom, understand that she needed the reassurance of his love beyond that room?

She knew that a marriage forced by an unplanned pregnancy wasn't the best groundwork on which to build a relationship. But she'd loved Clayton from the moment she'd met him, and that love had only grown stronger through their first year together. And though he'd never once professed his love for her, seemed hesitant to display any kind of affection at all, she'd sensed deep in her heart that he cared for her. She'd never tried to conceal her feelings for him, hoping that, by her example, he would feel more comfortable in displaying his.

But he hadn't. Instead, with the passing of the years, he'd become even more withdrawn, spending more and more time away from home. Away from her.

Through a blur of tears, she watched him swing

his truck around, its headlights slicing a beam of light through the darkness. She watched until the trailer's red taillights disappeared down the drive, then she dropped her forehead against the glass and wept.

Early-morning sunshine drilled ruthlessly at Clayton's eyelids, punching him from a deep sleep. Groaning, he shifted on the seat, stiff from having spent the night behind the wheel of his truck. Unable to find a more comfortable position, he gave up on the idea of getting any more sleep and forced his eyes open. He stared dully through the windshield for a few minutes, slowly becoming aware of his surroundings. And with awareness came remembrance of why he was there.

He turned his head to look out the side window and focused on the front porch of Rena's house. He'd come back only hours after their last conversation, knowing there was one last thing he had to do for Rena. A dull ache slowly spread through his chest as he envisioned her as she'd stood there the night before, tears streaming down her face. He closed his eyes against the memory, but he couldn't stop the voice that had haunted his sleep from playing through his mind again.

There is no "us," Clayton. We don't have a relationship. We never have. We simply share an address and a bed, when the mood strikes you....

I had dreams and plans for my life, too, Clayton, the same as you did for yours, but I put my dreams aside when we married and moved to the ranch, while you went right on chasing yours.

He groaned and dropped his forehead to his palms, slowly wagging his head. Robbed her of her dreams?

He snorted a rueful laugh. She didn't even know the worst of it. If she did, she'd despise him all the more. And with good cause. For not once, in all the years of their marriage, had he even considered the possibility of her *having* dreams, much less her losing them, nor had he ever given any thought to what sacrifices she might have made when she was forced to marry him.

To his credit he *had* thought about the material things she'd given up. Worried about them, even. So much so, that he'd doubled his efforts at rodeoing and on the ranch, working hard to provide her with the finer things she was accustomed to having. He'd never wanted her to regret that she'd had to marry him. Had never wanted to give her cause to leave him.

And now she was leaving him, anyway.

Tears stung his eyes, blurring his view of the house as he angled his head to peer at it again. He wanted to be angry with the woman inside, but found he couldn't. Didn't deserve the emotion. Not when he'd cost her her dreams.

The hell of it was, he thought as he stared miserably at the house where she now slept, he didn't even know what dreams he'd robbed her of. He'd spent a good part of the night trying to think what it was that she might have sacrificed for him and the kids, but hadn't been able to come up with one blessed thing. Sad to admit that a man knew so little about his own wife. Sadder still to think that he hadn't even realized she was unhappy.

Dragging the back of his hand across the moisture that had gathered in his eyes, he reached for his hat and snugged it over his head as he shouldered open the door and slid to the ground. Wondering how he could have been so blind, so selfish, when faced with such kindness and love, he pulled his sunglasses from his pocket and pushed them on, studying the house through the dark, protective lenses, while he looked for a sign that Rena and the kids were up. But the house was still as a church house on Saturday night, not so much as a flutter of movement appearing behind its smudged and dirty front windows.

Not wanting to try to rouse Rena for fear of waking the kids so early, he rounded the trailer to check on his horse. The gelding stood at the side of the trailer where Clayton had tied him the evening before, his eyelids at half-mast, a rear hoof cocked as he balanced his weight on three legs. "Hey, Easy," he murmured, lifting one hand to scratch the horse between the ears as he untied the lead rope with the other. "Let's see if we can find you a place to graze for a while."

Gathering the rope in one hand, he led the horse around the trailer and to a gate he'd noticed the day before. After leading the horse inside the fenced area, he unfastened the rope from the halter, then gave the horse a parting pat before closing the gate between them and heading for the front of the house.

Bracing his hands low on his hips, he stared at the house long and hard and finally concluded that a couple of hours of sleep and bright morning sunshine did nothing to improve his first impression of the place.

It was still a dump.

Wondering why Rena would want to move the kids to a rat hole such as this one, he walked around the side of the house, examining the structure, his confusion growing when he became aware of even more repairs that needed to be made.

As he rounded the rear corner of the house, the back door opened, and he stopped, then drew back into the house's shadow when he saw Rena step out onto the porch, her hands wrapped around a thick mug of coffee.

The sight of her stole his breath.

His wife was one of those rare women who looked beautiful, made up or not…but to Clayton, she was never more beautiful than when she first woke up, a discovery he'd made the first morning he'd awakened with her beside him in bed. He knew she would never have believed him if he'd ever found the courage to share with her his secret, but there was something about seeing her with her eyelids still heavy with sleep, with the imprint of her pillow still creasing her cheek and with her hair sticking out all over the place that made him weak in the knees. Always had.

Fearing that, if Rena had her way, this might very well be the last chance he'd ever have to see her like this, he stood quietly and looked his fill.

The T-shirt she wore he recognized as an old one of his, hitting her about midthigh and exposing a long stretch of tanned legs. As he moved his gaze down their shapely length, he remembered her legs being one of the things he'd first noticed about her that night in Oklahoma City, when they'd first met. Dressed in a short suede skirt that showed off her legs to perfection, she'd smiled at him from across the width of a crowded dance floor. Though he had known full well that she was younger than him by a few years, and way out of his league, he hadn't been able to resist responding to the kick in the gut he'd felt when their gazes had first met.

Physical attraction. He'd experienced it before, but never as strongly as he had that night. One dance and he'd known by her body's response to his that he could have her. She'd melted against him in all the right places, drawing a response that was hard for either of them to ignore. He knew he could have walked away from temptation. Probably should have. Caught in similar situations, he had before. But for some reason he'd found that he couldn't walk away from Rena. And though their actions that night had changed his life forever, he'd never had any regrets.

But obviously she'd had a few.

Stifling a sigh, he let his gaze settle on her bare feet where her toes curled over the edge of the porch, then slowly moved his gaze back up, stopping at her chest when she inhaled deeply, dragging in a long breath of fresh morning air. Full and still erect, despite having nursed twins, her breasts swelled beneath the thin fabric, her nipples forming stiff, enticing peaks.

Wanting more than his next breath to sweep her up into his arms and carry her straight to the nearest bed and make love to her as he had just before dawn the morning he'd left Tulsa, instead he set his jaw against temptation and forced his gaze back up to her profile.

"Got any more of that stuff?"

Startled by the sound of his voice, she whirled, then swore, when hot coffee sloshed over the side of the mug, scalding her hand. Tucking her hand behind her back, she held it there and frowned. "I thought you'd left."

"Gave it some thought," he replied, crossing to the porch. "Even did, for a while. But changed my mind." Standing on the step below her, he met her gaze for a moment, then reached around her and caught her wrist, pulling her injured hand from behind her back. Holding it open between them, he felt the thrum of her pulse beneath his fingers, the tremble of nerves, and wondered if, in spite of all her denials, he might still be able to persuade her to come home with him. Taking a chance, he lifted her hand and dipped his head over it, pressing his lips against the burn.

He heard her sharp intake of breath, felt her pulse kick and slowly lifted his head to meet her gaze. But before he could name the emotion he saw swirling in her eyes, she dropped her chin, hiding them from him. When she lifted her face again, her brown eyes were cool, free of any emotion.

"What do you want, Clayton?"

Slowly he released her hand, feeling the disappointment settle over him. "Some of that coffee would be nice," he said, nodding toward her cup.

She hesitated, looking as if she wanted to refuse him, then turned for the door. "I'll bring you a cup."

With a sigh Clayton dropped down on the stoop and took off his hat, settling it over his knee. He glanced up as the door opened again, and accepted the cup she held out to him with a grateful sigh.

When she didn't make a move to join him on the stoop, he patted the weathered step beside him as he sipped at his coffee. "Take some weight off," he invited.

She hesitated a moment longer, then finally sank down beside him, drawing her own cup between her hands. They both stared out at the field behind the house, the silence between them growing more and more awkward. Rena was the one who finally broke it.

"Clayton?"

"Hmm?"

"I'm…I'm sorry for the things I said last night."

The apology took him by surprise, but he tried not to read anything into it that wasn't there. "You needed to unload. We all do from time to time. I'd say you were past due."

She dropped her gaze, staring at the cup she balanced on her knees. "But there was no need for me to be so…so cruel. This isn't all your fault. I share some of the blame."

Though he didn't dare hope, Clayton couldn't stop himself from asking, "Is there any chance that we could—"

She shook her head before he could finish, then inhaled deeply and lifted her face to stare out at the field again. "No," she said, blinking back tears. "It's best this way."

Though he wanted to ask who she thought it was best for, Clayton feared that if he did he'd only start another argument. And he didn't want to fight with her anymore…which only left one topic to discuss.

The details of their divorce.

Unable to bring himself to broach the subject, he glanced back over his shoulder to peer up at the house. "How much did you pay for this place?" he asked, hoping to buy some time with her by drawing her into conversation.

"The price was fair."

Shaking his head at her defensive tone, he dropped

his gaze to look at her. "And how would you know what fair was?"

"I'm not completely helpless, Clayton," she replied sharply.

"Didn't say you were," he said, determined to keep the peace. "I merely asked how you knew the price was fair."

"I did a market analysis, studying recent sales."

Unaware that she even knew what a market analysis was, he drew his brows together as he peered at her. "How'd you know how to do that?"

"I've done them before." She lifted her shoulder in a careless shrug. "During the summers, while I was in college, I worked at Dad's bank, in the real estate department."

Not having known that—another testament to how little he knew about his wife—Clayton set aside his cup and plucked his hat from his knee. Slowly he began to spin it by its brim, watching its slow movement. "Was that one of the dreams you gave up?" he asked quietly.

"To work for my dad?"

"Yeah."

She snorted a laugh, then took a sip of her coffee. "Hardly."

"What were they, then?"

She turned her head slowly to look at him. "You really want to know?"

"I asked, didn't I?"

She turned away to focus on something in the distance, a soft smile curving at her lips. "One was to have my own business."

"That's pretty broad. What kind of business?"

"Interior design."

"Is that what you studied in college?"

She drew back to look at him. "Design?" At his slow nod, she sputtered a laugh. "Heavens, no! My father would never have permitted me to pursue such a frivolous degree. He expected me to work for him after I graduated, which meant a major in finance."

"And you studied finance, just because he wanted you to?"

"Wanted me to?" she repeated, then shook her head. "Ordered would come closer to the truth."

Clayton stared at her, understanding a little better about the rules she had told him about, how she'd lived her life at someone else's direction.

"Mommy?"

Rena and Clayton both turned to look at the screen door where Brittany stood, sleepily rubbing her eyes. Rena set down her cup and jumped to her feet. "What, baby?" she asked in concern as she opened the door and stooped to pick up her daughter.

"I'm hungry," Brittany complained.

"Want a doughnut and some juice?"

Brittany reared back in her mother's arms, her lips pushed out in a pout, and plucked at the neck band of Rena's T-shirt. "No. I want eggs. And bacon."

"But the stove isn't hooked up yet," Rena reminded her as she gently smoothed her daughter's tousled hair from her face. "Remember? How about some cereal?"

Brittany ducked away from her mother's touch. "Don't like cereal," she said peevishly.

"Yes, you do."

Brittany dug a fist against her eye, her lower lip beginning to quiver. "Don't want cereal. Want eggs."

"But I can't cook eggs without a stove, Brittany," Rena told her patiently. "You know that. So which do you want? Doughnuts? Or cereal?"

The tears that had threatened turned into a full-scale storm. "I hate cereal," she wailed, arching her back and pushing against her mother's chest, in what looked to Clayton like the beginnings of a major temper tantrum. "I want eggs."

Seeing the frustration building on Rena's face and realizing a way to ease to it, as well as buy him a little more time with his family, Clayton climbed the porch steps. "Is it a gas stove?"

Rena nodded as she struggled to calm Brittany. "But the serviceman hasn't come to connect it, yet."

"I'll hook it up for you."

Rena glanced up at him over the top of Brittany's head. He could see the refusal in her eyes, but before she could voice it, he reached for the screen door. "Won't take me a minute, shortcake," he said, and gave Brittany a comforting pat on the back. "Then your mommy can cook you those eggs."

Five

Elbow-deep in dishwater, Clayton glanced over his shoulder as Rena returned to the kitchen.

"Is Brittany happy now?"

Wondering why he continued to linger, but reluctant to question him about it since he had been so helpful, Rena picked up a dish towel and plucked a plate from the drainer. "Yes. She and Brandon are watching cartoons." She dried the plate and stretched on tiptoe to place it on the shelf of the cupboard in front of her.

"I won't fight you on the divorce," he said quietly.

She snapped her head around to look at him, sure that she'd misunderstood. "What did you say?"

"I won't fight you on the divorce. And I'll do the filing, if you want."

Though she was the one who'd wanted the divorce, demanded it even, hearing Clayton's quiet acceptance of it made it more real somehow. More final. She sank back to her heels, swallowing hard, then glanced away and plucked another plate from the drainer to dry it. "That's not necessary," she murmured. "I will."

"Whatever," he said, lifting a shoulder in a shrug. "And you don't need to worry about me paying child support. I'll take care of my kids."

Rena swallowed again, harder this time, feeling the tears rising. "I never doubted that you would."

Frowning slightly, he placed another stack of plates in the sink. Silence hummed around them for several nerve-burning minutes, before he spoke again.

"When I was at the ranch," he said in a voice so low Rena had to strain to hear him, "I noticed that you only took the furniture from the kids' rooms and a few odds and ends around the house." He glanced over his shoulder at the card table she was using as a temporary dining table, his frown deepening as he returned his gaze to the dishes filling the sink. "You can have anything else you want. I have no need for any of that stuff."

"Okay," she said slowly, her hand shaking a little as she reached for another plate to dry.

"In fact," he said, angling his head to look at her, "you can have the whole damn house. You can sell this place and move back to the ranch. I can find somewhere else to live."

Though his offer was generous and seemingly sincere, Rena couldn't stop the resentment it drew. The house she'd purchased was more to her than simply a place to live. It represented her independence, her need to feel in control of her life. "I don't want the house. I told you that last night. My home is here in Salado now."

Sighing, he drew his hands from the dishwater, braced his forearms on the edge of the sink and dipped his head, dragging his forehead wearily across his sleeve. "I figured that's what you would say," he muttered.

"Mommy!"

Rena whirled at the panic she heard in Brandon's voice, then tossed down the dish towel and ran for the den. Clayton followed a step behind.

She burst into the room, her breath burning in her lungs, then stopped, when she saw that Brandon and Brittany still lay sprawled on the floor in front of the TV set, their chins propped on their fists, just as she'd left them earlier. "What's wrong?" she cried, not seeing anything out of the ordinary.

Brandon glanced over his shoulder. "The TV went off," he said, then turned and pointed at the dark screen. "See?"

Having assumed by the panic she'd heard in Brandon's voice that something dire had happened to one of the twins, she huffed a breath and marched across the room. "Don't ever scream like that, unless there's an emergency," she lectured firmly. "You nearly scared the life out of me." She stooped to pick up the remote control from the floor, then straightened, frowning. "You probably just hit the off button without realizing it," she said, aiming the control at the television set and punching the button. Her frown deepened when nothing happened, and she punched the button again several times. "The batteries must be dead,'' she muttered, and turned the control over to check them.

"Rena?''

She glanced up to find Clayton fiddling with the light switch by the door. "What?''

"I don't think it's the batteries.'' He turned to look at her, his expression grim. "The electricity's off.''

"Off?'' she repeated dully. "But how? It was on a minute ago.''

He shrugged. "Could be a fuse burned out, or you might have thrown a breaker. Where's the electrical box?''

"On the back of the house, I think.''

Clayton headed for the door.

"Where are you going?'' she asked, dropping the remote control and hurrying after him.

"I'm going to check the box.''

"Do you know how to do that?'' she asked, unable to hide the doubt in her voice.

He stopped suddenly, and Rena bumped against his back. Flustered she retreated a step, meeting his gaze when he frowned at her over his shoulder. "I'm not totally helpless,'' he replied dryly.

Hearing her own words tossed back at her, she tipped up her chin and brushed past him. "I didn't say you were. I just wasn't aware that you knew anything about electricity.''

"Seems there's a lot we don't know about each other.''

She stopped at the back door and turned to peer at him curiously.

He reached around her and pushed open the back door. "Amazing, isn't it?'' he said as he pressed a hand to the small of her back and nudged her through the doorway. "Married over four years, and we're more like strangers than husband and wife."

Her thoughts growing pensive, Rena led the way to the electrical box, then stepped back, watching as Clayton opened the small door and peered inside.

It was sad to think about, yet she knew what he had said was true. They were more like strangers than man and wife.

Shaking off the melancholy that that realization drew, before it could settle over her, she rose to her toes to peer over his shoulder. "Do you see anything wrong?"

He turned and held up an object.

"What is it?" she asked in confusion, staring at the small device he held.

"A fuse. A burned-out fuse, to be exact."

"Is that bad?" she asked worriedly, lifting her gaze to his.

"Not so long as you have another one to replace it."

She rolled her eyes. "Well, obviously I don't, since I didn't even know what it was. So what do I do now? Call a repairman?"

Shaking his head, Clayton tucked the fuse into his pocket and headed back for the house. "No need to call a repairman. I can replace it."

She stared at his back a moment, then hurried after him. "You have a fuse in your truck?"

"Nope." He held the door open for her. "But I can run into town and buy one."

"But weren't you planning on leaving?"

He pressed a hand against her back to urge her through the doorway. "I can't very well leave, knowing my kids don't have any electricity."

"Mommy?"

"In the kitchen, Brittany," Rena called, then turned back to Clayton. "How long will it take to replace it, once you have a new fuse?"

"About five seconds. A little push and a twist, and it's in."

Brittany skipped into the kitchen. "That lady called."

"What lady?" Rena asked, still trying to absorb the news that Clayton was staying a little longer.

"The baby-sitter one."

Rena immediately dropped to a knee in front of her daughter, dread filling her. "What did she say? Is she on her way?"

Brittany shook her head. "Nope. She said for me to tell you that she can't come today."

"What!" Rena cried. "But she has to come! I have appointments scheduled."

Clayton stood off to the side, listening and tuning in to the panic in Rena's voice and wondering what kind of appointments she had that the thought of missing them would upset her so much. "I can stay with the kids," he offered.

"Oh, no," Rena said, brushing off her knees as she stood. "I couldn't ask you to do that."

"They're my kids, Rena," he reminded her wryly. "It's not exactly a hardship to have to stay with them for a couple of hours."

With the twins strapped safely into the passenger seat beside him, Clayton drove slowly down the main street of Salado, keeping one eye peeled for a glimpse of Rena's Lincoln Navigator, still curious to know what kind of appointments she might have that would take more than half a day to complete.

Not that he'd made the trip into town to spy on her, he assured himself. He'd made the trip to buy a new fuse.

"Daddy?"

"Yeah, shortcake?" he murmured, while he scanned both sides of the street.

"Can me and Brandon have an ice-cream cone?"

He glanced down to look at his daughter. "Ice cream?" he repeated. "You had breakfast not more than two hours ago."

"I know," she said miserably, looking up at him with those huge, puppy-dog eyes of hers. "But I'm hungry, and so's Brandon."

Shaking his head at his daughter's habit of thinking and talking for her twin brother, Clayton turned his gaze back to the street. "I suppose you can, since you're both starving, though it might take me a while to find a place that sells ice cream."

Brightening, Brittany sat up, straining to see over the dash. "There's an ice cream store right across the street from Mommy's shop," she informed him. "We can get some there."

Clayton froze. "Mommy's shop?" he repeated slowly. "What shop?"

"The one where she works," Brittany explained, still straining to peer over the dash. "There!" she cried, lifting a finger to point. "That's the ice cream store."

Clayton followed the line of her finger, noting the location of the ice cream store, then shifted his gaze across the street, and saw Rena's Navigator parked on the drive beside a small, frame house. A sign

swinging from a post near the curb read By Design.
"When did your mother open a shop?"

"It's not open yet," Brittany told him, always a
wealth of information. "Can we go and see her, after
we get our ice cream?"

Clayton steered his truck into a parking space in
front of the ice cream store and killed the engine. "I
suppose," he said, his gaze on the side rearview mirror and the reflection of the little house across the
street, stunned by the discovery that Rena had
opened a business.

Clayton wasn't sure whether to knock on the front
door of By Design, or just walk in, but was saved
making the decision when Brittany twisted the door-
knob and barreled inside, followed closely by her
brother, both screaming, "Mommy, Mommy! We're
here!"

Drawing in a deep breath, Clayton followed. He
stopped just inside the door and glanced around, resentment and despair warring for dominance as he
noted the boxes stacked around the small front room,
wondering just exactly how long his wife had been
planning on leaving him.

"Hi, Clayton. What are y'all doing here?"

He glanced up as Rena walked into the front room,
flanked by the twins, who danced at her sides. Steel-
ing himself against the resentment that was quickly
winning the battle for control of his emotions, he
pulled off his hat. "We were in town, picking up the
fuse, and the kids wanted ice cream." He lifted his
hat to gesture toward the store across the street.
"Brittany knew where to find it."

Laughing, Rena dropped to a knee, wrapping her

arms around her children and drawing them to her sides as she pressed their cheeks against hers. ''She has the nose of a bloodhound when it comes to sweets.''

His resentment growing at the tender scene his family created, Clayton snugged his hat back down on his head. ''I'll get 'em out of your hair. I'm sure you've got important business to tend to.''

Rena glanced up at him, her smile fading at the resentment she heard in his voice. ''Not so busy that I don't have time to say hello to my children.'' She smiled down at the twins, gave them a tight squeeze, then lifted her gaze to Clayton's as she rose. ''Would you like a quick tour? There's not much to see yet. But I can show you what all I've got planned.''

The flush of excitement on her face sent a stab of jealousy through him, which was ridiculous, he told himself. He wasn't jealous of her new business, but he didn't want a tour of her shop, either. Before he could refuse her offer, though, Brittany shot across the room and grabbed his hand.

''Come on, Daddy,'' she said, tugging him along behind her. ''I'll show you the bathroom. It's got a tub with feet.''

Once Clayton got back to Rena's place, he settled the twins in front of the television and wandered through the house, still feeling a bit shell-shocked over the discovery that Rena had started a business without his knowledge. He wasn't being nosy, he told himself as he headed for the staircase. He was just curious to see what kind of condition the rest of the house was in. Keeping his steps as quiet as possible, he climbed the stairs to the second floor and peeked in the first door.

His heart twisted a bit when he saw that the twins' furniture and toys filled the room, arranged in much the same way as they had been in their room at the ranch. Not liking to think about that now-empty room, he turned away and continued down the hall, finding several bare rooms before opening a door and discovering Rena's bedroom.

The bed that dominated the large space was as big as the one they'd once shared, but the furnishings were dramatically different. Where their bedroom at the ranch had reflected more of a man's taste, this was one did anything but. From the eyelet fabric that skirted the bed, to the downy, white comforter that was spread neatly across its top and the tumble of pastel throw pillows artfully arranged at its head, this room screamed woman.

Resenting the differences, but unsure why, Clayton stepped into the room and walked around, noting the antique chifforobe and the lounge chair angled in front of a window, obviously placed there to catch the view of the rolling fields beyond. He stopped beside the round bedside table with its flounced cloth that hung clear to the floor and the fragile-looking, porcelain bedside lamp. Pushing a finger against the assorted knickknacks on the tabletop, he picked up a pewter frame, expecting to find a picture of the twins. He was shocked when he found instead an image of himself and Rena staring back at him.

Surprised that she'd chosen to display a picture that included him, he sank down on the bed, staring, trying to remember when the picture had been taken. Two or three months after their marriage, he supposed, judging by the size of Rena's already protruding stomach. Slowly he recalled more details as he examined the print more closely. There was a rodeo arena in the background—the one in Brady, Texas, if he remembered correctly. Pete Dugan had taken the shot, he recalled, insisting that Rena would need a picture of Clayton in order to remember his ugly face once the twins were born and she wouldn't be able to travel the circuit with him any longer.

He glanced out the window at the thought of Pete, his traveling buddy, with his off-the-wall sense of humor and mother-hen ways. Pete had fussed at Clayton more than once over the years, as had Troy when Clayton had failed to call home and check on Rena and the kids as often as Pete thought he should. And though Clayton had known Pete was right, he hadn't been able to make the calls, a fact that had infuriated Pete all the more.

But then, Pete hadn't known how hard it was for Clayton to make those calls, the history that kept him from exposing his heart and emotions to his wife and kids. If he had known, then maybe he'd have left Clayton alone or, at the least, quit beating Clayton up with his failings as a husband and a father.

Sighing, Clayton looked down at the picture he held, remembering those first few months of their marriage and how good they'd been. His thoughts drifted as he stared at his wife's radiant face, able to feel even now the warmth of the arm she'd hugged around his waist just before the picture had been snapped.

What went wrong? he asked himself. When did everything change? They'd been so happy, so content with each other. How had they lost all that?

He set the picture back on the table and rose, dragging a hand over his hair. When they'd first married, he was sure that he'd finally put his past behind him, had the beginnings of the family he'd always yearned for. Then the twins had come along and—

The phone rang, interrupting his thoughts, and he glanced at it, wondering if he should answer it. It rang again, and he muttered a curse under his breath as he reached for it. "Hello?"

Silence hummed for a couple of seconds before a woman said uncertainly, "I'm sorry. I must have dialed the wrong number."

Suspecting that it was hearing his voice that had made the woman draw that conclusion, Clayton asked, "Were you calling Rena?"

"Well, yes," the woman said in surprise.

"She's not here right now," he explained. "Could I take a message?"

"Please," the woman said, sounding relieved. "Tell her that Mrs. Givens called, and that I won't be able to keep the twins for her for at least another two weeks. My daughter in Houston is pregnant," she explained, "and is having some complications. Her doctor has ordered her to bed, which means that she needs me to stay with her, so that I can take care of her two-year-old."

"Okay," Clayton replied, slowly absorbing this news.

"I hope this doesn't put Rena in a bind," the woman fretted. "She's such a nice lady, and I know she was depending on me. But it just can't be helped," she said with a sigh. "My daughter needs me, and I simply can't be in two places at once."

Clayton glanced at the doorway, thinking of the

twins downstairs and Rena in town at her new shop, wondering how Rena would deal with this newest kink in her plans. "I'm sure she'll understand," he told the woman, wondering if fate might have just dropped in his lap the perfect excuse for him to hang around a little longer...and hopefully the time he needed to change his wife's mind about divorcing him.

"What!"

"Mrs. Givens can't start work for another two weeks," Clayton said again. "Her daughter's pregnant and—"

Rena sliced an impatient hand through the air, cutting him off. "I heard what you said," she said, then seemed to crumple, her eyes filling with tears. "What am I going to do?" she moaned, covering her face with her hands. "I'll never be able to find another baby-sitter on such short notice."

"I'm sure there is someone you could get," Clayton offered helpfully.

She jerked her hands from her face to glare at him. "Who? It took me weeks to find Mrs. Givens! And I've got so much to do yet," she said miserably, turning away from him. "The carpenter is coming tomorrow to build shelves and racks for my fabric samples." She began to pace, worrying her thumbnail. "And the painters are coming Friday to paint. I'd take the children with me, but I know I wouldn't get a thing done for worrying about them sticking a finger beneath a saw blade, or getting sick from smelling the paint fumes." She stopped and dug her fingers in her hair. "And there's so much yet to do!" she wailed.

"I could stay and keep them," Clayton offered quietly.

Rena dropped her hands to stare. "Stay?" she repeated incredulously. "Here?"

"Well, it only makes sense for me to stay at the house with y'all, since I'll be minding the twins."

"But, you can't!" Rena cried, already imagining the intimacy that would force them into. An intimacy that she was sure would drive her insane. She'd already proven to herself that she was weak where Clayton was concerned, and she knew she couldn't bear having her heart broken again.

"Why not? It's a big house. I'm sure there's an extra bedroom I could use. Or I can bunk in with the kids."

"But…but…"

"But what?"

She searched her mind, trying to think of an excuse that he would accept. "Your career!" she exclaimed on sudden inspiration. "You can't just drop off the circuit this close to the finals."

He lifted a shoulder in a shrug, then turned to stir the stew he had simmering on the range for their dinner. "I can afford to miss a rodeo, or two."

"No," she said, pressing her fingertips against her temples, unable to bear the thought of the pain, the frustration, that his nearness would cause her. "Clayton, you can't stay here. It just wouldn't work."

"And why not?"

"Because…" She firmed her lips, refusing to share with him her reasons. "Just because."

"Well, there is one other option."

"What?" she demanded to know, sure that anything would be better than sharing her house with Clayton.

"I could pack up the kids and move them back to the ranch with me for a while."

Rena fell back a step, the blood draining from her face. "No," she whispered, shaking her head. "You can't do that. You can't take the children away from me. I'm their mother. They need me."

He hit the spoon against the side of the pot, knocking off the vegetables that clung to it and making Rena jump. "Why not?" he asked, tossing the spoon to the counter as he turned to face her. "You're taking them away from me. And they need a father just as much as they need a mother, so don't try that particular argument again, it won't—" He stopped, narrowing his eyes at her, and slowly brought his hands to his hips. "Now that I think about it, maybe I ought to just take them back to the ranch with me for good. I have a right, you know. They're my kids as much as they are yours."

Rena stared at him, panic threatening her ability to breathe. She'd never considered that he would fight her for the children. And if he did, would a judge grant him full custody? It seemed ridiculous to even consider, what with Clayton on the road so much of the time, but she'd heard of other cases where parents had fought over custodial rights and the months, sometimes years, it took to settle the issue...and not always in the mother's favor.

Sickened by the thought of putting the twins through the emotional tug-of-war a fight for custody would result in, and sobered by the thought that she might not win if Clayton did fight her for them, she turned away and wrung her hands as she tried to think of a way out of the predicament she'd placed herself in.

Realizing that he had her up against a wall, with no options other than the ones he'd offered, she turned to face him again. "I'm sorry," she said, and forced a regretful smile. "Of course you can stay here. I'm just tired, is all. I overreacted. It's been such a long day."

Though he looked as if he wanted to debate the issue with her a little longer, to her relief he dropped his hands from his hips and turned back to the stove. "Fine. I'll bring in my gear after supper."

After checking on the children one last time, Rena started down the hall toward her own room at the opposite end. Noticing that a light still burned in the room she'd assigned to Clayton, she slowed her steps, unable to keep from stealing a glance into the room as she passed by. What she saw dragged her to a stop.

Barefoot and wearing nothing but his boxers, Clayton stood in the center of the room, his back to her, shaking the wrinkles from his bedroll. Guilt that she hadn't been able to supply him with a proper bed to sleep in tried to worm its way inside her…but there simply wasn't room. Lust had already filled the space.

She'd always admired her husband's body. Lusted for it, if she were to be truly honest. The wide shoulders, narrow hips, muscled legs. Even now as she stared at him, knowing she should turn away, she couldn't seem to tear her gaze from the sight of the muscles rippling on his back, the rounded swell of buttocks beneath the boxers, the dark hair that shadowed his legs.

"Did you need something?" he asked.

Unaware that he had turned his head to peer at her, she jerked her gaze to his. Her face burning in embarrassment at being caught staring, she shook her head. "No. I was just on the way to my room and I saw you—" she gestured helplessly at his bedroll "—making your bed." Aware that her hand was shaking, she dropped it to her side and curled it into a fist. "I'm sorry that I don't have a proper bed to offer you, or, at the very least, a sofa. I've ordered furniture. It just hasn't arrived yet."

Clayton snorted a laugh and gave the bedroll one last shake, before whipping it out and holding it by two corners as it settled over the floor. "I've slept in worse conditions. At least I won't have to listen to Troy snore."

At the mention of Troy, Rena momentarily forgot her embarrassment, and a wistful smile curved her lips as she took a step into the room. "How is Troy? I haven't talked to him in ages."

Clayton lifted a shoulder. "Fine, I guess. Last I heard he was headed for New Mexico with Yuma." He cupped a hand around the back of his neck and rubbed, frowning. "He's been having a run of bad luck lately. Hasn't picked up any winnings in several months."

"Oh, no," Rena murmured sympathetically, knowing the effect a string of losses could have on a cowboy's confidence, as well as on his bank balance. "That's too bad."

"It'll change, though," Clayton assured her. "A streak of bad luck can only last so long."

"Do he and Pete know about…" Unable to complete the question, she dropped her gaze.

"About us?" Clayton asked. At her slow nod he scowled and tossed the pillow he'd picked up onto his bedroll. "Yeah. In fact, Pete's at the ranch right now, keeping an eye on things for me."

Rena snapped up her head, her eyes wide in alarm. "But Carol—"

Clayton nodded, his scowl deepening. "Yeah, I know. I asked him if her living right next door, and all, was going to cause him a problem, and he assured me it wouldn't."

But it might create a problem for Carol, Rena thought, thinking of the secret Carol had shared with her, the secret Carol had kept from Pete for two years. Not even Clayton was aware of the small grave on the hill behind Carol's house.

She didn't realize that she'd allowed her concerns for her friend to show on her face until Clayton said, "No need to worry, Rena. They're both adults. They can take care of themselves."

She forced a smile. "Of course they are," she said, then frowned as another thought occurred to her. "But why did you ask Pete to stay at the ranch? Rubin can handle the work alone. He has for years."

"He could if he wasn't home in bed with the chicken pox," Clayton replied wryly.

"Chicken pox!"

"Yep. Said he caught it from his kids."

"Oh, no," Rena moaned, sagging weakly.

Clayton was across the room in two long strides to catch her by the elbows, sure that she was going to faint. "Oh, no, what?"

She lifted her gaze to meet his, her eyes filled with

tears. "Brittany and Brandon haven't had the chicken pox."

"So?" he said in confusion. "I'm sure there are a lot of childhood diseases they haven't had yet."

"But they've been *exposed* to the chicken pox," she cried, frustrated that he didn't understand. "They played with Rubin's children the day before we left for Oklahoma."

He tightened his grip on her, his fingers digging into her skin. "What's the gestation period?"

"I'm not sure," she said, sniffing. "Ten days, I think."

"Ten days," he repeated slowly, and mentally counted backward. He dropped his head back with a groan, having done the math.

"I know," she said, her eyes filling with tears again. "They could break out anyday now."

Hearing the fear in her voice, and knowing that he was only feeding it by revealing his own, Clayton forced a confidence to his voice as he shifted her to his side and slung an arm around her shoulders. "So what if they do? Chicken pox is part of growing up," he reminded her as he walked with her down the hall to her own bedroom. "All kids get it, eventually."

Rena stopped just outside her door and looked up at him. "Have you had them?"

"Well, uh— No," he finally admitted.

Tears spurted to her eyes again. "What if you catch them from the twins? Chicken pox is much worse on adults, than it is on children."

Not having thought of the danger of becoming infected himself, Clayton slowly absorbed that possibility. He hated being sick. Always had. But he couldn't let Rena see his apprehension. She was scared enough as it was. Hoping to hide his own worries from her, he hooked an arm around her neck and drew her face to his chest. ''Come on, now,'' he said gruffly, smoothing a wide palm down her close-cropped hair. ''I'm not going to get sick. Hell,'' he said, hoping to tease her from her gloomy thoughts. ''My hide's too thick. There isn't a germ around strong enough to penetrate it.''

He felt her shoulders hitch in a laugh beneath his arm, and he released a long breath, relieved that his teasing seemed to have worked.

She sighed and wrapped her arms loosely around his waist. ''I'm glad you're here, Clayton,'' she murmured. ''If the twins should break out with chicken pox, I'm not sure that I could take care of them alone.''

Clayton stilled his hand's movement on her hair as she relaxed against him, suddenly and painfully aware of the breasts pressed against his chest, the heat where her abdomen burned against his groin. Wondering if she was even conscious that she was in his arms, he closed his eyes and drew her closer, wanting to savor the moment.

He wasn't sure how long he held her—a minute, maybe two, could've been ten, for all he knew—before she slowly lifted her head from his chest. He glanced down to find her face tipped up to his, her lips slightly parted, her eyes wide and dark with the same burning awareness that hummed through his veins.

Before he could stop himself, he had lowered his face over hers and covered her mouth with his. He lost himself immediately in the sweetness...then was slowly dragged under by the fire that rose to engulf him. He lifted his hands to frame her cheeks, holding her face to his, though she seemed no more eager than he to break the kiss.

He angled his face to the side and took the kiss deeper, wanting, no, needing more of her. He felt the almost-desperate dig of her nails into his back, worried about it...then sighed inwardly as her grip on him eased. He felt the tremble in her hands as she smoothed them up his back, was humbled by it, then groaned when she curled those same trembling hands around his neck and pulled his face closer to hers.

A hunger surged to life within him, and he took that first bold step, backing her toward her bed. At its side he reached behind her and ripped back the downy comforter, scattering pillows, then stripped down the top sheet. He never once broke their kiss. Didn't dare, fearing that if he did he might break whatever spell she seemed to be under, and she would demand that he stop.

Careful not to startle her, he placed a hand low on her back and leaned his body into hers, guiding her down and following to cover her body with his. Every curve beneath him was so heartbreakingly familiar, every swell so seductively sweet. Filling her mouth with a low groan, he shifted to wedge a knee between her legs.

And that's all it took to break the magical spell.

The fingers at his neck tensed, her nails scraping against his skin, and her body, once soft and pliant, stiffened beneath his. A heartbeat later, her hands were no longer at his neck, but were wedged between them and pushing at his chest.

"No," she moaned, tearing her mouth from his and turning her face away. "Don't. Please."

Bracing a hand on either side of her head, Clayton lifted his chest from hers to stare down at her. ''Don't?'' he repeated in confusion.

She rolled her head from side to side, then squeezed her eyes shut...but not before he saw the tears there.

''Rena?'' he said, stunned by them. Her breath hitched, and he rolled to her side, gathering her into his arms. ''I'm sorry, baby,'' he soothed, stroking a hand down her hair. ''I thought you wanted—''

She shook her head again as she eased from his embrace and sat up, sniffing. ''This is why I didn't want you here,'' she admitted tearfully.

''Why?'' he asked, more confused than ever.

Groaning, she tipped her face to the ceiling and curled her hands into fists against her thighs. Thighs that, a moment ago, had lain beneath his.

''I don't want just sex from you, Clayton,'' she said angrily.

''Well, what exactly do you want?'' he shouted, his anger rising to meet hers. ''It's not as if I *forced* myself on you. As I recall, you were right there with me, matching me beat for beat.''

She drew in a long breath and opened her palms against her thighs in a obvious struggle for calm. ''Yes, and I shouldn't have. I'm sorry.''

He bolted from the bed. ''Sorry?'' he shouted, glaring down at her. ''Sorry?'' he said again, unable to believe she thought she could salve his wounded pride, mend his broken heart, with something as frivolous as an apology. ''Well, I'm sorry, too,'' he told her. ''Sorry that I tried to offer you comfort. Sorry that I read your signals wrong. Sorry that I offered you sex, when you obviously don't want it or anything else from me.'' He drew in a deep breath, prepared to continue his list of things he was sorry about...but blew it out in a frustrated huff of air, instead. ''Just forget it,'' he muttered and whirled for the door. ''I won't make the mistake of touching you again.''

Six

It took longer than usual for Rena to dress the next morning. Swollen eyes from a night spent crying were difficult to conceal.

She'd known from the moment that Clayton had suggested staying at her house that she was in trouble. Any woman who had experienced a sexual relationship as satisfying as hers had been with Clayton would find herself in the same predicament Rena now faced. Living under the same roof. Sharing the same space. Breathing the same air. The attraction seldom ended with the relationship. Rarely, if the woman still loved the man. Never, if the man happened to be Clayton.

And though she knew she could slip easily back into a physical relationship with Clayton, one that promised sexual satisfaction, the kind of relationship that he seemed content enough with, Rena wanted so much more. She wanted his love.

Unfortunately, that wasn't what he'd offered.

Dreading facing him again, she walked downstairs and into the kitchen and found him already there, standing before the stove, his hair tousled, his feet bare. Dressed in only faded jeans that rode low on his hips, he sipped at a cup of coffee while he transferred crisp strips of bacon from a frying pan to a platter. With each lift of his hand, muscles rippled across the wide expanse of his bare back, drawing her gaze. She stopped, staring, her mouth drying up, her nerves sizzling right along with the bacon in the frying pan.

The temptation was there, just as she'd known it would be. Even feared. She knew how easy it would be, so natural, really, to cross the room and splay her hands over his back, feel the play of muscle beneath her palms. He would turn. Gather her into his arms. Their lips would meet. Tease. The heat—

Giving herself a shake, she pushed the image back and forced herself into motion. "Good morning, Clayton," she said briskly as she headed for the coffeepot.

He glanced over his shoulder, his expression unreadable, then returned his gaze to the stove. "'Mornin'."

"I would've cooked breakfast," she said as she poured herself a cup of coffee. "It wasn't necessary for you to."

"I don't mind cooking."

"Still…"

"I said I don't mind," he repeated, and wiped a

hand across the back of his jeans before picking up the platter. "Should I wake the kids?"

Though she wished the children were awake, if only to serve as a barrier between Clayton and her, she shook her head. "No. Let them sleep. They didn't have a nap yesterday, and I'm sure they're tired."

Glancing at her, he slid the platter onto the counter behind her, then shifted his gaze away to pull down two plates from the cupboard, frowning. "Was I supposed to put 'em down for a nap?"

"Yes—no." Flustered by his closeness, she eased a step away before turning and watching him serve eggs onto a plate. "Yes, you were. But it isn't your fault. I forgot to tell you."

Still frowning, he speared a couple of slices of bacon and added them to the plate. "Anything else I need to know?"

Distracted by the swell of bicep, the play of tendons along his arm, she had to force herself to concentrate on his question. "Brittany likes to dress herself, though she has a tendency to choose her very best clothes. That's fine, as long as she doesn't play outside in them."

"Okay. What else?" he asked, and began to fill the second plate with food.

"You'll need to monitor the TV shows they watch. If the program's at all scary, change the channel. If you don't, Brandon is sure to have nightmares."

He picked up both plates, turned, then stopped, eyeing the rickety card table with distaste. Making a quick detour for the back door, he beckoned with his chin for her to follow.

Once outside, he dropped down onto the stoop, waiting until she was seated beside him before passing her a plate.

Sure that she couldn't swallow anything past the knot of yearning in her throat, Rena picked up her fork and pushed at her eggs. "If something comes up that you can't handle, you can call me. I left the number for the shop on the pad by the phone."

"I'm sure we'll get along just fine."

"There's a first aid kit in the twins' bathroom upstairs."

"I doubt we'll need it."

"Well, if you should…"

"Then I'll use it."

Hearing the resentment in his voice, she sighed, knowing that she must sound like the world's biggest worrywart to him. "I've never left them before," she said softly as she set aside her plate.

"You did yesterday."

"Yes," she admitted, feeling the tears rising. "But for some reason it seems so much harder to do today."

"Why?"

She shook her head. "I don't know. Maybe reality is setting in. I'm used to being at home with them. Picking up after them and cooking for them, settling their disputes when they fight." She laughed, realizing how ridiculous that sounded. "Imagine missing all of that."

"You'll get used to it. 'Fore long, you won't even remember the way it was before."

She turned to peer at him. "Did you?"

"What?" he asked, glancing her way.

"Forget what it was like to be at home with the twins?"

He stared at her a moment, then set his jaw and looked away. "No. I never forgot."

"Are you mad at us, Daddy?"

Pulled from his contemplations of his conversation with Rena, Clayton angled his head to look at Brittany, where she sat perched on the tailgate of his truck alongside her brother, both watching him groom Easy. "No. Why do you ask?"

"You're wearing a mean face."

He snorted a laugh and went back to brushing Easy. "I'm not mad. Just thinkin', is all."

"What about?"

He angled his head to look at her again. "You writin' a book?"

She shook her head. "I don't know how to write yet."

Chuckling, he tossed the brush into the tack box and untied the horse. The kid always had an answer—and it seemed a hay barn full of questions. "Y'all want to ride Easy back to the pasture?" he asked, hoping to distract Brittany from her questions.

Both twins scrambled to their feet. "Can we?"

He led Easy alongside the tailgate and tossed the end of the lead rope over the horse's neck. "So long as you keep your feet still," he warned and snagged an arm around Brittany's waist. He swung her up onto Easy's back, then turned for Brandon, but stopped when he noticed Brandon's flushed cheeks. He placed a knuckle beneath the boy's chin and tipped up his face. "You feeling okay?" he asked uneasily.

At Brandon's slow nod, Clayton dropped his hand, telling himself he was getting as bad as Rena. The boy had probably just had a little too much sun, he told himself, then caught Brandon under the arms and swung him up behind Brittany. "Hang on to your sister," he instructed, and pulled the lead rope from around Easy's neck.

"Can we go fast?" Brittany asked, filling her hands with the horse's mane.

"Not without me up there with you to see that you don't fall off."

"Oh, pooh," Brittany scoffed. "We won't fall off, will we, Brandon?"

Before Brandon could verify her claim, Clayton shook his head. "We'll take a ride some other time. You kids have had enough sun for one day. Besides, it's time for your nap."

Clayton led the horse to the pasture, ignoring Brittany's muttered complaints about not being tired and only babies needing naps. After helping the children down, he removed Easy's halter and gave the horse a pat before herding the twins out the gate.

"Daddy?" Brittany asked as they walked back up to the house.

"What, shortcake?"

"Do you have a mommy and daddy?"

Clayton faltered a step at the question, but quickly recovered. "No."

"Not ever?"

"Well, yeah. Everybody does. But mine died when I was little."

"Did you have to go live in an orphanage when they died, like Little Orphan Annie did?"

"No," Clayton said, shaking his head slowly, not

wanting to think about those years. "I lived with relatives."

"What relatives?"

"Well, with my grandparents, at first, until they got too sick to keep me. From there I went to live with my uncle Frank and his family. After a couple of years, they shipped me off to live with Aunt Margaret and her brood."

"Did they put you in a box?"

"Box?" he repeated, stopping to peer down at Brittany in confusion.

"To ship you in," she explained. "When Mommy ships stuff to Nonnie and Pawpaw, she always puts it in a big box."

Chuckling, Clayton strode on to the house. "No, they didn't put me in a box."

"How come you lived with so many people?" she asked after a moment.

Clayton lifted a shoulder. "Nobody wanted to keep me on permanent, I guess."

"Were you bad?"

"No. Not particularly. I reckon they just had too many kids of their own to want another one around."

He felt a hand slip into his and glanced down to see Brittany looking up at him. "I'd keep you, Daddy," she murmured sympathetically. "Even if you were bad."

Not wanting to think about the memories Brittany's questions had drawn, and needing something to do to fill the time while the twins napped, Clayton dug a screwdriver and hammer from the toolbox he kept in his truck, and set to work on the cockeyed shutters that framed the house's front windows. He tightened the screws on one, after pulling it back into place, replaced a missing screw on another, then stepped back to examine his work. Pleased with the improvement he'd made, he worked his way around the first floor of the house, methodically righting all the shutters.

He'd just stepped back onto the front porch, when the screen door squeaked open and Brandon appeared.

"You already awake, son?" he asked in surprise.

Brandon rubbed his eyes and nodded. "I'm hot, Daddy."

His gut clenching in dread, Clayton tossed the screwdriver into the toolbox and crossed to Brandon, hunkering down to press a palm against his brow. "I'll say you are," he muttered, and hauled the boy up into his arms. "Let's get you in the tub and see if we can cool you down."

He pulled open the door and let it slam behind him as he loped up the stairs, taking them two at a time. When he reached the children's bathroom, he turned on the water in the tub, then began stripping off Brandon's clothes.

"You feel okay?" Clayton asked as he settled the boy in the water.

Brandon stretched out his legs and rubbed a hand across his chest. "Yeah. Just hot."

Clayton knelt down beside the tub, watching Brandon's hand move across his small chest, afraid to look and afraid not to. "Let me see," he said and gently nudged Brandon's hand aside so that he could get a clear view of the boy's chest. Seeing a red spot, he angled the boy toward him for a better look. "Do you itch?" he asked, finding a couple more red spots.

"Kinda."

"Try not to scratch," Clayton warned, and picked up a cloth. "It'll only make it worse." After dipping the cloth into the tepid water, he gathered it into his fist and squeezed water over Brandon's chest. "That feel better?" he asked.

Brandon nodded slowly. "A little."

"What are y'all doin'?"

Clayton turned to find Brittany standing in the doorway. "Giving Brandon a bath." Dipping the cloth into the water again, he lifted it and squeezed the water over Brandon's back.

"It's not time for bed yet," Brittany said, crossing to stand beside the tub. "How come you're giving him a bath?"

Not in the mood for another string of Brittany's questions, Clayton struggled for patience. "Because he's hot."

"I'm hot. Can I take a bath, too?"

"Hot?" Clayton cried in alarm, spinning on the balls of his feet to look at her. Seeing nothing on her face to indicate a fever, he pressed a hand against her forehead, sagging with relief when his palm met only cool skin. "You can take one after Brandon," he told her, and turned back to tend to his son.

"But I want a bath now," she whined.

"I said, after Brandon," he replied, putting a little steel behind his response.

Brittany dropped down on the floor. "But I want to take a bath, too," she wailed.

With his comfort zone already stretched to the limit bathing Brandon and his mind focused on how best to care for his son, Brittany's wail shot Clayton's tolerance over the edge. "I said no!" he shouted.

Wide-eyed, Brandon looked up at him, then leaned to peer over the side of the tub, watching his sister's tantrum growing in volume and intensity. "She can take a bath with me," he said, looking back up at Clayton. "I don't mind."

Though tempted, Clayton shook his head, knowing it wasn't wise. If Brittany hadn't already contracted chicken pox, a bath with Brandon was a sure guarantee that she would. "No, son. She can—" He frowned and glanced back toward the door, straining to hear over Brittany's continued wails. "What was that noise?"

"I think somebody's knocking on the front door," Brandon offered quietly.

"What next?" Clayton muttered under his breath. When the pounding continued, he heaved a sigh and stood to yank a towel from the towel rack. Scooping Brandon from the tub, he wrapped the towel around him, then hooked an arm around the still-wailing Brittany and tucked her under his other arm. His lips thinned in anger, he headed for the stairs and stomped down them. Kicking a boot at the screen door, he knocked it open. "What do you want?" he growled, holding the door open with a wide shoulder.

The two men standing on the porch took a step back, gulping. They shifted their gazes uneasily from Clayton's angry face to Brittany, then to Brandon, and finally back to Clayton. One of the two held up a clipboard. "We're here to deliver furniture to a Ms. Rena Rankin."

Groaning, Clayton dropped his chin to his chest,

wondering what else could possibly happen to complicate this day.

"Clayton! What's wrong?"

He glanced up to find Rena running across the yard, and had his answer when he saw the alarm on her face. "I was giving Brandon a bath," he explained, having to raise his voice to be heard over Brittany's crying, "and Brittany came in and wanted to take a bath, too."

He paused when Rena held out her hands to take Brittany, and scowled when Brittany fell into her mother's arms, sobbing. Rena quickly shifted the child to one hip and pressed Brittany's face into the curve of her neck, trying to calm her.

Sighing, Clayton shifted Brandon to a more comfortable position in his arms, then gestured toward the two men who waited, seemingly hanging on his every word. "About that time these two guys showed up. And—"

Rena turned to look at the two delivery men. "Do you have my furniture?" she asked hopefully. At their nods she sagged with relief. "Thank heaven. We've been eating our meals off a card table, and have had to sit on the floor to watch TV. Follow me," she said, gesturing to the two men, "and I'll show you where to put everything." Shooting Clayton a quelling look, she pursed her lips as she brushed past him. "You should have just let Brittany bathe with him," she muttered for his ears only. "I bathe them together all the time."

"Well, I would have," he replied indignantly, hefting the towel-wrapped Brandon higher on his hip as he followed her inside, "but I was afraid she would get chicken pox."

Rena whirled, her eyes going wide. "Brandon has chicken pox?"

The two delivery men backed slowly from the porch, then turned and bolted for their truck.

"As best I can tell. He's running a fever and has a few spots. Which was why I didn't want Brittany in the tub with him," he added wryly.

Rena thrust Brittany at Clayton, exchanging her daughter for her son. Balancing Brandon on her hip, she cupped a hand at his cheek. "Poor baby," she soothed, and pressed her lips against his forehead, then drew back to look at him. "Show Mommy your spots."

Brandon unwrapped the towel to expose his chest. "Here," he said, pointing. "And here."

"Where do you want the furniture, Ms. Rankin?" one of the deliverymen asked.

She glanced up to find the deliverymen had unloaded her new sofa and were standing on the other side of the door, straining beneath its weight. "Oh, I'm sorry. It goes in—"

"What are chicken pox?" Brittany asked, her tears miraculously gone.

"It's a disease, sweetheart," Rena said distractedly as she pushed open the door for the deliverymen.

"Is Brandon going to die?"

Rena whipped her head around to find Brittany looking at her, her eyes filled with fear. "Of course not!" she exclaimed, hugging Brandon to her chest, then leaned to press a kiss on Brittany's cheek. "He's just going to have a few red spots and itch for several days."

"Where do you want us to put the sofa, ma'am?"

Rena waved an arm toward the den. "In there. Anywhere, really. My husband can help me arrange the furniture later."

Clayton sat on the new sofa with his head tipped back against the plump cushions and Brandon cradled against his chest, only half listening as Rena read to the children from a book of nursery rhymes.

My husband, she'd said while directing the deliverymen. Though he was sure her use of the phrase was merely a slip of the tongue, he liked hearing her say it. Made him feel needed, still a part of this family.

"I think they're asleep," Rena whispered.

Startled from his thoughts, Clayton lifted his head and glanced down at his son's sleeping face, then shifted his gaze to Brittany who sat curled against her mother's breasts, her eyes closed, her thumb hanging slack from the corner of her mouth.

"Think it's safe to put 'em to bed?" he asked uncertainly.

"Yes, I think so."

Clayton shifted Brandon to hold him against his chest and stood, offering Rena a hand to help her to her feet. "You go first," he whispered, nodding toward the stairs. He waited for her to pass by, then followed her to the second floor.

He laid Brandon down on one twin bed, while Rena settled Brittany on the other, then pulled the covers to the boy's chin.

"Mommy?"

Clayton turned to see Rena sinking down on the edge of Brittany's bed. "What, baby?" she whispered.

"Do I have the chicken pox, yet?"

Smiling, Rena smoothed Brittany's bangs from her forehead. "No. Not yet."

"When will I get 'em?"

"I don't know. Maybe never. Daddy's never had them."

Brittany shifted her sleepy gaze to Clayton's. "Never?" she asked him.

He shook his head. "Never."

Smiling, Rena leaned to give Brittany a kiss. "Sweet dreams, sweetheart. Mommy loves you."

"I love you, too, Mommy," she murmured, yawning. She drew the covers to her chin, then looked up at Clayton. "'Nite, Daddy. I love you."

When Clayton didn't reply, Rena glanced over her shoulder and found him standing, staring down at Brittany, his lips in a hard line, his jaw set.

"Clayton," she prodded.

He glanced at her, stared a moment, his eyes dark, then turned away and headed for the door. "'Nite, shortcake," he muttered gruffly.

Shocked, Rena watched him disappear into the dark hall. "Mommy?"

Rena glanced back down at Brittany. "What, sweetheart?"

"Does Daddy love me?"

She leaned to press a kiss against her daughter's forehead. "Of course he does," she reassured her.

"But he never says he does. Not even when I tell him that I love him."

Her heart breaking because she understood her daughter's doubts so well, Rena cupped a hand at Brittany's cheek and smoothed a thumb beneath her eyelashes. "Your daddy loves you. I know he does.

Some people just can't say the words as easily as others.''

"Do you suppose it's because his mommy and daddy never taught him how?''

Frowning, Rena replied slowly, "Well, I don't know. Maybe.''

"He was little when they died.'' Brittany rolled to her side, nestling her cheek against her pillow. "He lived with a bunch of different people.''

Rena had known that Clayton's parents were deceased, but she hadn't known that other part of his background. "How did you know that?''

"Daddy told me. Nobody wanted to keep him,'' she added sadly. "And he wasn't even bad. He lived with his grandparents, till they got sick. Then with his uncle Frank, and after that, his aunt…somebody. I forget her name.'' She lifted her head from the pillow. "Do me and Brandon have any uncles and aunts?''

Sobered by all that Brittany had told her, Rena shook her head. "No. In order for you to have aunts and uncles, your daddy or I would have to have had brothers and sisters, and we don't have any.'' As soon as the words were out of her mouth, she glanced toward the door Clayton had disappeared through, wondering if she'd spoken the truth. For all she knew about his past, Clayton might have twelve brothers and sisters.

Sighing, she turned back to Brittany and leaned to drop one last kiss on her cheek. "No more talking,'' she ordered gently. "It's time to go to sleep.''

Closing her eyes, Brittany snuggled her cheek deeper into the pillow. "Okay, Mommy.''

* * *

After leaving the twins' bedroom, Rena headed downstairs in search of Clayton. Not finding him in the house, she stepped out onto the front porch, searching the darkness for a sign of him. When she heard the familiar pinging sound of grain hitting a metal bucket, she headed for the horse trailer, sure that she would find him there.

"Clayton?"

He glanced up at the sound of her voice, then slowly closed the side door of his trailer where he stored Easy's feed. "What?"

"I need to talk to you."

"About what?"

"About what just happened upstairs."

He turned away and headed for the pasture. "What happened?"

"What happened?" she cried, unable to believe that he was so insensitive that he wasn't even aware he'd hurt Brittany's feelings. "I'll tell you what happened," she said, charging after him. "You just broke your daughter's heart."

He swung the bucket over the fence and slipped the rope attached to it over a fence post. "And how did I do that?"

"She told you that she loved you and you didn't tell her back."

"I said good-night to her," he said defensively, avoiding her gaze by adjusting the rope on the post.

"But you didn't tell her that you loved her!" She pressed her fingers to her temples and inhaled deeply, silently praying for the patience to say what she needed to say without losing her temper. "Children need constant assurance from their parents that they are loved," she told him carefully. "Especially children whose parents are going through a divorce."

"I love my kids."

"And how do they know that, unless you tell them?"

"I take care of 'em. I provide 'em with a home and food and clothes and whatever else they take a liking to."

"But do you *tell* them? Do you ever say the words 'I love you'?" When he didn't respond, when he kept his back to her, she cried, "Clayton, do you?"

He whirled and she staggered back a step, stunned by the ravaged look on his face. "No. But I love 'em." He drew a fist against his chest. "With all my heart, I love those kids."

Her hand trembling, she reached to close a hand over the fist he held against his chest and squeezed her fingers around it. "Then tell them, Clayton. Tell them how you feel. Don't make them wonder. Don't ever give them a reason to doubt your love."

He jerked his hand from hers and turned away. "I can't."

She stared at his back, unable to believe she'd heard him correctly. "Can't? But why? If you love them, surely you can tell them that you do."

She waited for his answer, willed him to answer, to offer any plausible explanation for his inability to verbalize his feelings. But he didn't say anything. Not a word. He simply drew his hands to his hips and tipped his face up to the night sky. She watched the fabric on his shirt stretch across his back as he hauled in a long breath, heard the shudder in it when he finally released it.

And remembered what Brittany had said.

*Nobody wanted to keep him. And he wasn't even
bad.*

Certain now that his past had something to do with
his inability to verbalize his feelings for his children,
she closed the distance between them, laid a palm
against his back and leaned to peer up at him.

In the moonlight she could see the hard set of his
jaw, the rigid, flat line of his lips…the unshed tears
that glistened in his eyes. Her heart breaking at the
sight of them, she eased to his side and slipped her
arm around his waist.

"Brittany told me about you being moved around
a lot when you were little," she said softly.

Already tense, at her comment his body stiffened
even more.

"I've never tried to keep my past a secret."

"But you've never shared it with me, either," she
reminded him gently.

He rolled a shoulder. "My life was nothing like
yours, if that's what you're wondering."

"Tell me about it," she urged, then added,
"Please? I want to know."

He heaved a sigh. "My parents died when I was
a baby. In a car wreck. I don't remember them. Don't
even have a picture to know what they looked like."

She tightened her arm around his waist, hearing
the pain in his voice and knowing how difficult it
was for him to share this with her. "And your grandparents took you to live with them," she prodded,
wanting, needing to hear it all.

"For a while. They were old, sick. Too sick to
take care of themselves, much less a kid. When I
was about three, they shipped me off to live with my
uncle Frank. I stayed there till I was about five."

Rena watched the tears build in his eyes, saw how hard he struggled to fight them back.

Blinded by her own tears, she hugged him against her side. "I'm sorry. So sorry."

Not wanting her pity, Clayton stepped from her embrace and moved to the fence. Bracing his hands against the top rail, he dug his fingers into the wood and dipped his head, not wanting to remember. Unable to do anything else.

He felt Rena's hand on his back again and knew that he would have to tell it all. She wouldn't stop pestering him until he had. Resigned to that fact, he lifted his head and narrowed an eye at the moon, seeing it all as if it had happened only yesterday.

"He took me to the bus station and bought me a ticket. Parked me on the curb to wait for the bus that would take me to my aunt Margaret's. Everything I owned was stuffed into a grocery sack he dropped at my feet. I remember watching him walk away. Can still almost taste the sick fear that knotted in my gut. I didn't know what was happening, really, or where I was going. Too little to understand, I guess. All I knew was that Uncle Frank was leaving and when he did I was going to be alone.

"I yelled for him to wait, but he kept right on walking, never so much as looked back. I started running. Stumbled and fell a few times. Scrambled up and ran some more. I caught up with him at his car and grabbed ahold of him, crying and begging him not to send me away."

He paused, narrowing an eye against the memory, against the tears, before he could go on. "He backhanded me. Knocked me a good two feet or more, and I landed on my butt. I remember staring up at him, blubbering like you wouldn't believe, telling him that I loved him. That I'd be good. Begging that sorry son of a gun to take me back home with him.''

He shook his head, unable to believe even now what had happened next. "He grabbed me by an arm and jerked me up. Shook me till my teeth rattled in my head, then spun me around and shoved me back toward the bus station, telling me I wasn't his responsibility anymore.''

"Oh, Clayton,'' Rena cried softly. "I can't imagine anyone treating a child so cruelly.''

He snorted and glanced down at her. "By that time I was used to it. Didn't know any other way.'' He turned his face back to the sky. "He had a son. Bobby. A year or so older than me, I guess. Uncle Frank loved football. He'd sit in this big recliner and drink beer, watching it on TV for hours. Sometimes Bobby would climb up on his lap and Uncle Frank would wrap an arm around his waist and haul him up against his chest and they'd watch TV together. Seems ridiculous to think about it now, seeing as how bad Uncle Frank treated me, but I always wanted to sit up there, too. Tried to a time or two. Got the hell knocked out of me every damn time.''

"Oh, Clayton,'' she moaned tearfully. "I had no idea.''

"And why would you? I've never told anybody any of that stuff. Not even Pete and Troy.'' He angled his head to the side to look down at her and drew in a deep breath. "But you wanted to know why I can't tell the kids that I love 'em. Well, there's your answer. I don't know how. Scared that if I try, I'll screw it up, just like I did with my uncle Frank.''

Rena laid a hand against his cheek. "But you want

to tell them. I know you do. I've seen the way you look at them. The words are there in your throat, almost choking you. You just never let them out.'' Feeling the emotion clotting in her own throat, she drew her fingers to his lips. ''You don't have to hold back with Brittany and Brandon, Clayton. They love you. They would never intentionally hurt you.''

''Any guarantees come with that?''

Rena stared at him, knowing that she couldn't make promises that weren't hers to make. ''Give them a chance, Clayton. Don't hold back anymore. If you feel like doing something or saying something, then do it.''

When he straightened and turned to face her fully, she drew back, startled by the intensity with which he looked at her. ''What?'' she asked uneasily.

But he offered no reply, no explanation. He merely caught her hand in his and drew her to him.

Frightened, she braced a hand against his chest. ''Clayton! What are you—''

But before she could finish the question, he'd wrapped his arms around her, lifted her off the ground and closed his mouth over hers. He drained the fear from her with lips moist and demanding, then filled her with heat with a tongue that speared between her lips and plundered, leaving her weak and needy. Helpless to do anything else, she looped her arms around his neck and clung as his lips softened to brush across hers. She almost wept as his taste filled her, a taste she knew she would never forget, feared that she would always yearn for.

He loosened his arms around her and let her slide down his body, never once breaking contact with her mouth. Her feet touched the ground, and he eased his arms from around her to cup his hands at her waist and slowly pulled his mouth from hers.

Dazed, she inhaled deeply, savoring the kiss, then slowly opened her eyes to meet his gaze. "What was that for?" she asked breathlessly.

"You told me if I felt like saying something or doing something, I should just do it." He lifted his shoulder in a self-conscious shrug. "I felt like kissing my wife."

"Oh," she murmured, surprised that he'd followed her advice. "Oh-h-h," she said more slowly, realizing that Brittany and Brandon might not be the only ones affected by their father's past.

He drew his hands from her waist and stepped back, stuffing his hands deeply into his pockets. "I guess we'd better head back in," he said, gesturing toward the house with his chin. "Something tells me we're going to have our hands full tomorrow."

Seven

Rena tried to suppress the disappointment she'd felt when Clayton had released her and stuffed his hands into his pockets before walking with her back to the house...but failed miserably. She'd foolishly hoped that after their discussion everything would miraculously change, that Clayton would suddenly be freer with his emotions, more demonstrative with the children. And with her. But he wasn't. Granted, he had shared with her parts of his past that he'd never shared before and had acted on impulse by kissing her. But then he'd stepped away, stuffing his hands in his pockets...and, it seemed, his emotions right along with them.

Stifling a sigh, she glanced up from the order forms she was completing to look at Clayton, who sat across the room, a spool of hemp caught between his boots, slowly plaiting the strands into what looked to be a halter. Brandon lay on the floor not far from him, engrossed in a TV program.

Sighing again, Rena put her pen back to paper.

"Daddy? Will you read me a story?"

Rena glanced up again at Brittany's request to find her daughter leaning against Clayton's knee. She continued to watch, curious to see how Clayton would respond. She saw his hesitation, nearly wept over it, then quickly dropped her gaze back to her work, when he cut a glance her way. Praying that he wouldn't refuse Brittany, that he would take advantage of the opportunity their daughter was offering him, she held her breath.

She heard a rustle of movement and peeked over to see Clayton setting aside his rope and creating a space on his lap for Brittany. With tears burning in her eyes, she watched Brittany climb onto her daddy's lap, then twist around, plop down and push a book into Clayton's hand.

Clayton took the book from her, hesitated a moment, then wrapped an arm around her waist and tugged her back against his chest. Rena saw the flush of color on his cheeks, the tension in his body, and knew how difficult even that small display of affection must be for him.

Clearing his throat, he opened the book and began to read. "Once upon a time—"

"Skip that page," Brittany said and took the book from him, flipping pages, "and get to the good part."

Clayton glanced toward Rena, caught her watching, then shook his head, chuckling as he took the book from Brittany again and began to read.

"The mean stepmother didn't like—" He stopped again when a small hand settled on his thigh. He glanced down to find Brandon standing beside the chair, looking up at him. Shifting Brittany to one side, Clayton patted his thigh. "Climb on up, cowboy. There's room for you up here, too."

Smiling through her tears, Rena took up her pen again, telling herself that the little scene she'd just witnessed was a major breakthrough, and that she'd been foolish to expect a miraculous, overnight change in Clayton's behavior. After all, a lifetime of suppression couldn't be altered in a single day. It would take time.

At the thought she glanced up again to peer at Clayton, panic niggling at her earlier confidence. But would he have the time? How much longer would he be able to stay before he was forced to return to the rodeo circuit in order to maintain his place in the rankings and his chance to win another world championship?

Four days after Brandon broke out with the chicken pox, Brittany succumbed to the disease. Where Brandon had only developed a handful of spots, Brittany was almost immediately covered from head to toe…and nearly impossible to deal with. She whined, complained, cried and scratched, until Rena's nerves were raw from trying to keep her daughter happy and medicated.

Exhausted after only the first frustrating day following Brittany's breakout, Rena accepted Clayton's offer to rock their daughter to sleep. She collapsed onto her own bed, rolled to her side and was instantly asleep. Four hours later she awoke and sat up, blinking the sleep from her eyes and wondering if it had been a noise that had disturbed her. Hearing nothing, she slipped from her bed and tiptoed down the hall, needing assurance that it wasn't a cry from Brittany that had awakened her.

She stopped in the doorway of the twins' room, her heart melting at the sight that greeted her. Moonlight spilled through the bedroom window. In its beam sat Clayton, still in the rocker, with Brittany curled against his chest. His head was tipped back and he was sleeping with one arm wrapped loosely around Brittany's waist.

Her heart squeezing at the tender scene, Rena crossed the room and, unable to resist, swept the hair back from Clayton's forehead and pressed a kiss there. His eyes opened at her touch, his gaze shooting to hers. She smiled tenderly and let her hand drift to cup his cheek. "You need to go to bed," she whispered softly.

His eyelids drifted closed and he sighed, pressing his cheek against her palm as she stroked a thumb along the dark circle beneath one eye. Then, with another heavier sigh, he opened them again. "Just let me put her to bed."

"Here," Rena offered, "give her to me. I'll tuck her in. You're exhausted." After shifting Brittany into Rena's arms, Clayton mumbled a good-night and headed for the door. Rena watched him until he disappeared into the dark hallway, then, with a sigh, settled Brittany in her bed, waiting for a moment, until she was sure that her daughter didn't awaken.

As she walked back down the hall to her room, she paused at the door to Clayton's. Though dark inside, there was enough moonlight spilling through the window to illuminate his long form stretched out on the sleeping bag.

As she looked at him, she thought of all the things that he'd done to help keep the children entertained over the past few days, the easiness with which he had begun to respond to them. She envisioned him as she'd found him earlier, sitting in the rocker with Brittany curled against his chest, and she wondered about his own childhood, curious if anyone had ever rocked him when he was sick, if anyone had ever soothed his hurts.

Tears stung her throat as she realized the answer, and she crossed the room to kneel down beside him. Though she'd kept her footsteps light, had made no noise that would have alerted him of her presence, he must have somehow sensed her nearness. He lifted his arm from over his eyes and peered up at her. Long seconds passed as they stared deeply into each other's eyes, then he lifted the sheet from his chest, inviting her to join him.

Knowing full well what all she was gambling, Rena slipped beneath the covers and curled her body against his. With her head resting on his shoulder, her hand over his heart, she closed her eyes against the tears that threatened. "I love you, Clayton," she whispered.

She felt him raise his head, and lifted her own to meet his gaze. She saw the surprise in the blue depths, the emotion, and didn't wait for an answering response from him. She no longer needed one. He'd proved his love a thousand times over the past few weeks. She didn't need to hear the words.

Seeing his hesitation and understanding it, after all the pushing away she'd done, she braced her hand against his chest and shifted higher, placing her face opposite his. She caught his lower lip between her teeth, then opened her mouth over his, welcoming him in as freely as he'd welcomed her into his bed.

On a low groan he closed his arms around her and drew her over his chest, matching her length to his. With a hand cupped at the back of her neck, he took over ownership of the kiss and swept his tongue lightly across her lips, then crushed his mouth over hers.

Rena had known passion with Clayton, but she'd never tasted, never experienced anything like this. He seemed desperate to devour her, consume her. His hands swept over her back, down her legs, then back up, tugging her nightgown to her waist, baring her bottom. He filled his hands with the soft flesh of her buttocks and pressed her to him, grinding his already-hardening arousal against her.

When that closeness seemed only to frustrate him, he caught her nightgown in his hands and yanked it up, breaking their kiss only long enough to rip the gown over her head. Then his lips were on hers again, crushing, demanding, ravaging, and he was rolling her to her back and pressing his body over hers. His hands found her breasts and closed around them, squeezing, and her breath caught in her lungs and burned, as fire shot to her middle and pooled there. Before she could release the breath, he drew his hands to the very tips of her breasts, catching her nipples between his thumb and finger and lengthening them. She bucked beneath him, gasping, aching for the feel of his mouth there.

As if he'd read her mind, knew her thoughts, her needs, he dragged his lips from her mouth and down the column of her throat, shifting his body lower over hers. He lifted his head to meet her gaze, then captured her breasts between his hands and drew them together. With his gaze fixed on hers, searing her, he flicked his tongue over first one nipple, then the next, then closed his eyes on a low moan and opened his mouth fully, drawing her deeply inside.

Nearly wild with need, Rena fisted her hands in his hair and held him to her, thrusting her hips against his in a desperate search for satisfaction. When she was sure that she'd go mad from the passion clawing its way through her, he slipped a hand between her legs and found her center.

She bucked, gasping, and thrust her hips high... and almost wept in frustration when his fingers merely stroked the length of her and back up again, teasing her.

"Clayton. Please!" she cried. "I need you. Now. Please. Now."

With an agonizing slowness that she was sure was meant to drive her crazy, he pulled his mouth from her breast, then dipped his head to lap at the throbbing peak as he rose to brace himself above her. Shifting his gaze to hers, he positioned himself between her legs, then slipped a hand beneath her hips and guided her to him.

She arched, sobbing at the first contact, then gasped again as he plunged deeply inside her, shooting her high and over the edge. She grabbed his arms, curling her fingers around his corded biceps, digging her nails into his taut skin, clinging to him as pleasure washed over her in wave after wave after wave that threatened to drag her under.

He held her hips against his while her feminine walls throbbed around his length, then slowly withdrew, only to thrust again, harder and higher. Certain that she had experienced the ultimate climax, she clamped her eyes shut, crying out, as the waves rose higher, sweeping over her again, this time drawing her under. Each thrust of his hips against hers pushed her deeper and deeper into the darkness until she could no longer breathe, only cling.

"Come with me," he whispered, his voice raw with his own need.

Unable to speak, unable to form the words needed to tell him that she was too weak, too sated to move, she rolled her head against his pillow.

"Now, Rena," he whispered and thrust one last time, holding her against him. She dug her fingers deeper into his flesh as an explosion like nothing she'd ever experienced ripped through her. She felt the muscles in his arms grow rigid beneath her fingers, felt the strain of his body pushing against hers, heard the low groan that rose from deep inside him, then the delicious, pulsing heat of his climax as he filled her with his seed.

Sobbing, she lifted her arms to wrap them around his neck, and drew him down to her. His chest hammered against hers as he struggled to breathe, and he buried his face in the curve of her neck, pressing a wide hand against her cheek to hold her face against his. "Rena," he whispered, warming her flesh with his breath. "My Rena," he said on a sigh.

Rena didn't want to open her eyes, didn't want to lose the warmth of the body curled around hers, the memory of a night of wild mating. But a voice kept punching at her, refusing to let her cling to the delicious memories.

"Mommy! I'm hungry!"

She flipped open her eyes, just as Clayton lifted his head from the curve of her neck, his eyes reflecting the same horror that she knew must be mirrored in hers as he looked down at her.

She gulped. Swallowed. Then cleared her voice. "Okay, Brittany," she said, trying to sound natural, calm, when she felt anything but. "Why don't you and Brandon go downstairs and turn on the TV."

"Okay," Brittany said from the doorway, sulking. "But hurry. Me and Brandon are starving."

Rena closed her eyes, slowly counted to ten, then opened them again to meet Clayton's gaze. "Do you think they're gone?" she whispered. "Do you think they saw anything?"

He dropped his face to her neck again, to smother a laugh. "Yes, they're gone. And, no, I don't think they saw anything."

Rena shoved furiously at his head. "This isn't funny. I'm naked. And so are you, for that matter. What if they'd seen us? What would they think?"

Still chuckling, Clayton lifted his head and propped his cheek on his hand as he looked down at her. "They're only four. I doubt they'd think anything. Although now that I think about it," he said, sobering, as he shifted his gaze to a breast he'd exposed when he'd moved. "They might have nightmares." He slipped a hand over the breast, then cupped it. "Imagine the horror of seeing your mother naked. Naked," he repeated and dipped his head to lap at the rosy center, then shuddered. "It'd be enough to give any kid nightmares for weeks."

In spite of her embarrassment, Rena found herself closing her eyes on a sigh as he shaped his lips around her. "Don't," she whispered, weakened by the feel of his lips tugging at her nipple. "We've got to dress and get downstairs before Brittany comes looking for us again."

He groaned and drew her deeper inside his mouth. "You don't think we have time for just a little—"

"Mommy! We're starving!"

She opened her eyes at Brittany's impatient shout, meeting Clayton's startled gaze. "What do you think?" she asked, arching a brow.

"Don't scratch, Brittany," Rena ordered.

"But it itches," Brittany complained.

Hearing the frustration in both of their voices, Clayton pulled another pair of socks from Brittany's drawer and carried them to the bathroom along with a change of clothes for Brittany.

Fresh from an oatmeal bath, Brittany stood on the bath mat while Rena dried her. "Here," he said, and nudged the pair of socks against Rena's arm. "Put these on her hands. If she scratches, she can't do as much damage."

Rena looked up at Clayton in surprise as she accepted the socks. "That's a wonderful idea," she said, then turned to Brittany and smiled. "Look what daddy brought you," she said, tugging the socks over her daughter's hands. "Mittens to wear so that you won't make sores when you scratch."

"Those aren't mittens," she complained. "They're socks."

"Magical socks," Clayton said, dropping to hunker down beside Rena. "When you put 'em on your hands, they turn into mittens. See?" he said, holding up one of her hands for her inspection. "Mittens."

Brittany giggled. "You're silly, Daddy."

"Mommy?"

Rena turned to find Brandon standing in the doorway. "What, sweetheart?"

"Somebody's coming."

Rena rose, frowning. "Who?"

He shrugged and turned for the door. "I don't know, but there's a car coming up the drive."

Clayton gave her leg a pat. "Go on and see who it is. I'll finish up dressing this little critter."

"I'm not a critter," Rena heard Brittany say as she stepped out into the hallway. "I'm a little girl."

Laughing softly, Rena skipped down the stairs, feeling cheerful and fresh, in spite of the small amount of sleep she'd received the night before. The mere thought of her night with Clayton made goose bumps pebble her flesh. Shivering deliciously, she opened the front door.

What she saw made her blood run cold.

"Oh, no," she murmured under her breath as she stepped out onto the porch and watched the luxury car brake to a stop in front of her house. Feeling the dread building, she watched her father step from one side of the car, then shifted her gaze to watch her mother step from the opposite side. The look on her mother's face as she stared up at Rena's house said it all. In Gloria Palmer's eyes, her daughter had lowered herself to an all-time low.

Forcing a smile, Rena moved down the steps to greet her parents. "Hello, Mother," she said, dropping the expected kiss on her mother's cheek before turning to her father. "Hi, Dad," she said and gave him a kiss, as well. "I didn't know y'all were planning to come for a visit."

"I wanted to call first, but—"

Gloria waved a hand, silencing her husband, then caught Rena's hand in hers, the smile she offered as fake as her hair color. "We wanted to surprise you," she said, then puckered her lips in a pout. "You don't mind, do you, dear?"

Forcing a smile of her own, Rena withdrew her hand. "Of course not. Though it would have been nice—" She heard the front door of the house open behind her and saw the shock spread across her mother's face. She turned to see Clayton standing on the porch, balancing Brittany on one hip, Brandon on the other.

"What is *he* doing here?" her mother snapped peevishly. "And what is wrong with Brittany's hands? Has that brute harmed her?"

Before Rena could reply, Gloria was charging for the porch. "What have you done to that baby?" she cried, and reached to snatch Brittany from Clayton's arms.

But he spun, turning his back to her.

Brittany held up a hand as she peered over her daddy's shoulder. "They're magical socks, Nonnie," she explained, turning her hand this way and that. "When you put 'em on your hands, they turn into mittens."

"My God!" Gloria shrieked, having gotten her first look at her granddaughter's face. "What has happened to you? What is wrong with your face? And your arms!" she cried, when Brittany dropped her hand to wrap an arm around her daddy's neck. She whirled, furious. "Rena. What is wrong with her? And why is that *man* here? I thought you were divorcing him, which is exactly what you should do and should have done years ago.

"He's nothing but trash," she cried, then turned to gesture wildly at the house. "And he's dragged you down to his level with him. Imagine! A Palmer living in a place like this!" She pressed a hand at her breasts and inhaled deeply, then pressed her lips together and marched down the steps, scowling. "Well, you're not staying another minute in this house, and neither are my grandchildren. Martin. Go inside and pack their things. We're taking them all back to Oklahoma with us."

Clayton knelt to set Brittany down and then gave her a nudge toward the door. "You and Brandon go on inside and watch TV," he ordered. When he was sure they were out of earshot, he stood. "You're not taking my family anywhere."

Gloria stared at Clayton, her mouth sagging open. "How dare you speak to me in that tone of voice! You are nothing. *Nothing!*" she repeated, her voice rising to a shrill shriek. "Do you hear me? Nothing! I told Rena not to marry you. I warned her what would happen. She thought she could pull you up to her level, but you dragged her down to yours instead."

Clayton cut his gaze to Rena's. "Is that true?"

"Yes, it's true!" Gloria railed before Rena could answer. "I told her she should have an abortion. Told her that we would pay for it. But she chose to run off and marry *you* instead."

"Stop it!" Rena cried, unable to stand another minute of the war being waged around her. "Stop it! I don't want to hear another word from anyone."

"Oh, you'll hear more from me," her mother warned, shaking a finger at her daughter's nose. "I haven't said *near* all that I have got to say." She whirled to aim the same finger at Clayton. "And I'm not even close to telling you what I think of you, either."

Clayton stomped down the steps and shoved his face up close to his mother-in-law's, bracing his hands on his hips. "Say what you've got to say, then I want you to get the hell off this property."

"No!" Rena screamed, clamping her hands over her ears. "I won't listen to any more of this. I won't!"

Startled, Clayton tore his gaze from Gloria's and turned to watch Rena storm up the steps and to the front door. She glared down at the three adults standing in her yard, tears streaming down her face. "I'm sick of this!" she cried. "And I will *not* subject my children or myself to any more of this petty bickering. I want you to leave. All of you," she screamed, then ran inside the house, slamming the door behind her.

Clayton didn't wait around to see if the Palmers followed Rena's instructions. He loaded up his horse, said to hell with whatever belongings he'd left in the house and turned his truck and trailer for the ranch.

Fury, red-hot and blinding, fueled the first twenty or so miles of his trip. Anger carried him the rest of the way home. Rena had rebuked him. Sent him packing. And in front of her parents, no less.

He swore when his cell phone rang, then picked it up and pitched it out the open window. If it was Rena calling, he didn't want to talk to her. She'd made her feelings known when she'd ordered him to leave. He didn't need to hear any more. He'd received her first message loud and clear.

* * *

"Hey, buddy!" Pete shouted and headed for Clayton's truck just as Clayton climbed down from the cab. "I didn't know you were coming home." He clapped a hand on Clayton's back, then leaned to peer around him, looking inside the truck's empty cab. His smile slowly melted. "Where's Rena and the kids?"

Clayton slammed the door behind him. "Salado."

"Salado!" Pete echoed, turning to watch Clayton stalk toward the house. "What're they doing in Salado? I thought you were bringing them home?"

"Yeah, well, so did I. Seems Rena has other plans."

"Plans? What plans?" Pete put his feet in motion, jogging to catch up with Clayton. "Surely she isn't going through with the divorce?"

"Seems she is."

"Oh, man," Pete murmured sympathetically, clamping a hand over Clayton's shoulder and squeezing. "That's tough. Real tough."

Clayton shrugged free of his hand. "Where's Rubin? Is he still home sick?"

"No," Pete said slowly, eyeing Clayton warily. "He's back at work. I was just here collecting the rest of my gear from the barn."

"You headin' out for a rodeo?"

Pete shook his head. "No. As a matter of fact, I'm thinking about retiring."

"Retiring?" Clayton said. "What the hell for? We've got a couple of months yet to ring up some numbers before Las Vegas and the finals."

Pete shoved his hands into his pockets and scrunched his mouth to one side, while he dug a hole in the ground with the toe of his boot. "Yeah, I know. But Carol and I are getting married."

"Married!"

"Yep." Pete swelled his chest and pulled his hands from his pockets to give his belt a cocky hitch. "Finally came to her senses and decided she couldn't go on livin' without me. All but begged me to marry her on the spot."

Clayton snorted. "I'll just bet she did."

"Well, she did," Pete cried indignantly. "Ask her yourself."

Clayton shook his head and turned away. "Nope. I'm avoiding all females for a while."

"Where're you goin'?" Pete called after him.

"Gatherin' me some gear and hittin' the road." Clayton pulled open the back door to his house, then turned and shot Pete a wink. "I've got me some time to make up."

The phone was ringing when Clayton stepped inside the house. He stopped and stared at it for a minute, then walked over to the phone jack and ripped it from the wall. Dusting off his hands, he turned for his bedroom, telling himself that a man can only have his heart kicked back in his face just so many times, before he learned to quit putting it out there to have it kicked.

His uncle Frank had tried to teach him that lesson when he was five years old. He'd finally earned his degree at the ripe old age of thirty-four, under Rena's tutelage.

He supposed that just proved that his mother-in-law had been right all along. Clayton Rankin was nothing but a stupid cowboy.

Eight

Rena set the phone back in its cradle, then dropped her face to her hands.

"Was Daddy home?"

At Brittany's question she dragged her hands down her face, then dropped them to her lap to meet her daughter's gaze across the table. "No. I guess not. He didn't answer."

"Did you try his cell phone?" Brandon asked helpfully.

"Yes. No answer there, either."

Brittany pushed her lips out into a pout. "You shouldn'a made him leave."

"Brittany," Rena warned.

"Well, you shouldn'a," she said, folding her arms across her chest and sulking.

"I didn't want Daddy and Nonnie fighting anymore,'' Rena told her, struggling for patience. "I told you that."

"Maybe you shoulda just made 'em take a time-out," Brandon told her. "That's what you make me and Brittany do when we have a fight."

As miserable as she felt, Rena couldn't help but laugh at the image of Clayton and her mother sitting in Brittany's and Brandon's time-out chairs with their noses pressed into opposite corners. "Maybe I'll try that next time," she said, then added under her breath, "though I hope there isn't a next time."

"Call Pete," Brittany suggested. "I bet he knows where Daddy is."

"Or Troy," Brandon offered. "They're probably all together."

"I don't know," Rena said uncertainly. She really hated to drag Pete and Troy into the silent war Clayton was waging against her.

Brittany pushed the phone closer to Rena's hand. "Call 'em. I'll bet they can find my daddy."

Though Rena had vacillated for a good two hours or more, she finally broke down and dialed Troy's cell phone number while the twins were napping. She was shocked when a woman answered the phone. Thinking she'd misdialed, she said, "I'm sorry. I must have dialed the wrong number."

"Were you calling Troy Jacobs?" the woman asked.

Frowning, Rena said, "Well, yes. Who is this?"

"Shelby. Just a minute and I'll get Troy for you."

Stunned that Troy—shy, quiet, reserved Troy, who could rarely work up the nerve to ask a woman out—had a woman with him, Rena listened to Shelby call

Troy to the phone, her voice muffled by the hand she'd obviously placed over the phone.

"Hello?"

"Troy?"

"Rena?"

"Yes, it's me," she said, tears building at the sound of concern in his voice.

"Are you with Clayton?" he asked.

She pressed a hand against her lips and shook her head, then dropped it and drew in a deep breath. "No. In fact, I was hoping you might know where he is."

"No," he said slowly. "Haven't seen or heard from him in weeks. You might try Pete, though. He's probably still at y'all's ranch. He was looking after things while Clayton chased to Oklahoma to haul you and the kids back home." He paused, then said in a low voice, "Sorry. Didn't mean that to come out the way it did."

Rena smiled, though her eyes were filled with tears. "You don't have to apologize. That's exactly what he tried to do."

"Did y'all—that is to say, did you, well, uh—"

"Did we resolve our problems?" Rena asked, knowing how difficult it was for Troy to ask personal questions.

"Yeah. That. Did you?"

She shook her head, feeling the tears building again, then said, "No, not yet."

"If there's anything I can do…"

Rena pressed her hand over her mouth to stifle the sob that rose, then dropped it to her lap and balled it into a fist. "Thank you, Troy," she said, fighting back the tears. "You're a good friend."

* * *

After the emotional conversation with Troy, it took Rena two days to work up the courage to call Pete. She didn't waste her time calling him at the ranch, as Troy had suggested, because she knew that even if he was still there, she wouldn't get an answer. Either no one was at the ranch or Clayton had pulled the phone out of the wall. Knowing Clayton as she did, if it came to a bet, Rena was prepared to put her money on the latter.

She'd hurt him when she'd sent him away, but that certainly hadn't been her intent. She had just wanted the fighting to stop, and that was the only way she could think to end it.

Sighing, she picked up the phone and dialed Pete's cell number. It rang three times before he answered, saying "It's your dime. Talk to me."

She laughed, imagining Pete reared back with his chest all puffed out, his hat shoved back on his head, holding the phone tipped up to his mouth. "Pete Dugan," she teased. "It costs more than a dime to make a call these days."

"Rena?"

"Yes. It's me."

"Woman, you sure know how to stir up trouble when you put your mind to it."

Wincing at his sharp tone, she figured that he must have spoken to Clayton. "Yes, I suppose I do, though that wasn't my intent."

"Didn't say it was. Nor am I pointin' blame. I'm just sayin' that this is one hell of a mess you've gotten yourself into."

"I would have to agree with you on that point," she said miserably. "Is Clayton with you?"

"Nope. He's out on the road. Stopped by the ranch a couple of days ago, grabbed some gear and took off again."

"Did he say where he was going?"

"Can't say that he did. But I could probably find out for you. Give me your number, and I'll give you a call back."

Rena gave him the number and verified it once he'd written it down.

"Now I don't know how long it'll take me to track him down," Pete warned her. "This time of year there's lots of rodeos to choose from, and I'd bet my truck he's hittin' as many as he can."

"I understand. Just call me when you know something. It doesn't matter what time. Just call."

"Sure thing, darlin'. And you give those kids a hug from their uncle Pete. Hear?"

Rena smiled, remembering Brittany asking if she had any uncles or aunts. Hearing Pete refer to himself as one, made her realize that her children did have an uncle. Two, in fact. Though not by blood. "I will. And thanks, Pete. I owe you one."

"Chicken-fried steak," he said, naming his reward, and she could almost see his grin. "You always made the best."

"Chicken-fried steak it is," she said smiling. "Find Clayton for me, and I'll cook you a platterful."

Rena sweated through another day of pacing by the phone, waiting for Pete's call. When it finally came, she was fast asleep.

Awakened by the sound of the phone ringing beside her bed, she fought back the covers and grabbed for it.

"Hello?"

"Rena? It's Pete. I found him. Had to track him through three states, but I found him."

She sat up, brushing her bangs back from her forehead. "Where is he?"

"At the ranch."

"The ranch!" she cried. "But I thought you said he was out on the road."

"I did. And he was. But he's home again. And sick as a dog. Caught the chicken pox from the kids, from what I could gather, though he's talking out of his head and not makin' a whole helluva lot of sense. Fever, I guess. They say it's worse on adults than it is on kids."

Rena slid to the side of the bed and dropped her feet over the side. "Did you see him? Is he all right?"

"Are you kiddin' me? You know what Clayton's like when he's sick. You can't get within a mile of him. Grouchier than an old bear. That's what he is. And about as approachable as a rattler."

Rena sputtered a laugh, knowing that Pete wasn't exaggerating by much. "Yes. I know."

"Now I'm not tryin' to tell you what to do or nothin', but if I was you, I'd hightail it over to the ranch and check on him. Carol and I tried, but he won't let us in the door. Has himself barricaded in y'all's bedroom."

A fleeting concern about her shop darted through her mind, but Rena quickly pushed it aside. Clayton meant much more to her than her new business or her bid for independence. "I will," she said without hesitation. "First thing in the morning I'll pack up the kids and head for the ranch."

"Well, now," Pete said slowly, "I don't think you ought to be takin' those kids in with you. No tellin' what Clayton might say or do. Little ears, you know? Drop 'em at Carol's. We'll look after 'em for you."

Rena bugged her eyes. "*You're* with Carol?"

"Yep," he said, and she could just see him swelling his chest as he shared that bit of news. "Sure am. But I can go you one better than that."

Unable to imagine anything more surprising than Pete and Carol being together again, she said, "Okay, I'll bite. What?"

"Troy's married."

"What!"

"Yep. Got himself hitched to a pregnant, preacher's daughter."

"No," she said, shocked by the news. "I don't believe you."

"It's the God's truth. I swear. Though he's not the father of her baby."

Rena dropped her forehead onto her palm. "Pete. You're not making sense."

"I know. Blows your mind, don't it? But it's the truth, I swear. He met this woman in a café while he was out on the road, and she asked him to marry her so that her baby would have a name, and all. Gave him five thousand dollars in exchange for his name."

"She *paid* him to marry her?"

"Well, sorta. She gave him the money, but Troy never cashed the check. Listen, Rena. I gotta run. Carol's gettin' that come-hither look in her eye, and I need to take advantage while she's in the mood."

There was a scuffling sound, then a click, and the connection broke.

Chuckling, Rena leaned to hang up the phone, then sank back on her bed with a sigh. She was going to see Clayton in the morning. She was really going to see Clayton.

She brought her thumb to her mouth and started worrying her nail, wondering if she'd even get past the front door.

He would forgive her, she told herself confidently as she rose to start packing. Once she was able to explain why she'd asked him to leave, he would understand.

Wouldn't he?

Rena tried the front door first, found it locked, then walked around to the rear and used her key to enter the house through the kitchen door.

"Clayton?" she called uneasily, feeling the need to warn him that she was there. When he didn't respond, she headed down the hall that led to the master bedroom. She twisted the knob and pushed against the door...but it wouldn't budge. Frowning, she realized that Pete hadn't been exaggerating when he'd said that Clayton had barricaded himself inside.

"There's more than one way to skin a cat," she muttered, and headed for the kitchen and the back door. Once outside she walked around the side of the house and stopped before the master bedroom window. As she'd hoped, the window was still open a couple of inches, just as she'd left it.

She braced her hands beneath the sash and shoved the window up higher, then crawled through the opening, pushing her way through the closed drapes.

Standing in front of the window, she looked around. The room was cloaked in darkness, every drape closed against the sunlight, and a stale, sour smell hung in the air. Wrinkling her nose against it, she glanced at the bedroom door, found a chair shoved beneath the knob and frowned as she turned her gaze to the bed.

Clayton lay sprawled on his stomach across it, naked as the day he was born. She eased closer to examine his backside and found that the familiar red spots covered him from shoulder to waist. Emitting a sympathetic moan, she leaned to place a hand at the base of his neck...and noticed the perspiration beading his skin. Surprised that he would be perspiring when the temperature in the room was rather cool, she slipped her hand to his forehead, her eyes widening as heat burned against her palm.

Dropping to a knee, she swept his hair from his forehead to study his flushed face. "Clayton?" she said nervously. "Can you hear me? Wake up, sweetheart," she urged.

He moaned and turned his face from beneath her hand, and dropped his opposite cheek against the bed.

"Clayton, please," she begged, feeling the panic rising. "Open your eyes and talk to me."

When he still didn't respond, she climbed up onto the bed and crawled over his back to kneel beside him. "Clayton!" she cried, giving his shoulder a hard shake. "Talk to me!"

She watched his eyelids slowly lift, exposing dull, sightless eyes that slowly seemed to find focus. Slower still, he lifted his face, dragging his gaze up her body until it locked with hers. He stared a long, nerve-burning minute, then dropped his head back to the mattress, slamming his eyelids shut again.

"Get out," he growled.

Startled by the anger in his voice, Rena drew back, staring at the rigid set of his jaw. She'd known that he probably wouldn't be happy to see her, prepared herself for that eventuality, but she'd never once considered that he would order her to leave.

She firmed her lips and glared down at him. "I'm not going anywhere. I'm here to take care of you, whether you like it or not."

He flopped his head over, turning his face away from her again. "I don't need taking care of. I can take care of myself."

"Oh, and you're doing a marvelous job of that," she snapped. "When was the last time you changed the sheets?" she asked, eyeing with distaste the wrinkled and soiled bed linens.

"None of your damn business," he muttered.

Ignoring his resentful tone, she crawled across his back again to glare down at him. "Have you seen a doctor?"

"Don't need a doctor."

"Yes, you do, though I know you're too stubborn to ever admit it."

"Get out."

She pushed herself from the bed and grabbed the corner of the fitted sheet, ripping it from beneath the mattress. "I'm not leaving, so you might as well save your breath. Now, get up," she ordered, "so that I can change the sheets."

He rolled to his side to level a look on her that would have sent Satan himself running for cover. Rena merely lifted her chin. "Up," she repeated, then turned for the bathroom. "I'll run you a bath, and you can bathe while I change the linens."

Scowling, Clayton slid down into the cool water, listening to the sounds of Rena bustling around in the other room. He didn't want her there, he told himself. Wanted her as far away from him as she could get. Wanted her...

He groaned, fisting his hands at his temples to still the pounding in his head. His head had ached for days. His heart longer than that. But he didn't want her with him. Didn't want her taking care of him. Not when she'd already made her feelings for him more than clear.

"Does your head hurt?"

Unaware that she'd slipped into the bathroom, Clayton dropped his hands from his head and turned his face away to stare at the glass blocks that formed the window beside the tub, determined to ignore her.

He sensed more than saw her sit down on the side of the tub, and he drew his shoulder tighter against his chest, not wanting to accidentally touch her.

"How long has it been hurting?" she asked softly and smoothed her hand across his brow.

He closed his eyes against her cool, soothing touch and had to struggle to suppress the moan of pleasure her fingers drew. "Days," he said, feeling himself weakening as she continued to stroke his brow.

"When did you break out?"

"Two days ago, best I can figure. Spots are all on my back."

She drew her hand down his temple and along his cheek, her fingers brushing lightly beneath his eye. "Have you taken anything for the pain?"

"No."

Her hand disappeared from his cheek, and he opened his eyes to watch her cross to the vanity opposite the marble tub and dig through a drawer until she found a bottle of aspirin. Shifting his gaze to the mirror in front of her, he stared at her reflection while she filled a glass with water, his heart squeezing in his chest as he saw the tears that filled her eyes

"I'm gonna be okay, Rena," he said gruffly, feeling the need to reassure her. "It'll run its course, and I'll be good as new in no time."

She turned back to the tub and opened her hand, sniffing as she offered him the aspirin. His gaze on hers, he took them, then downed the glass of water she passed to him. Sighing, he set the glass aside, then caught her hand and pulled her down to the side of the tub again as he sank lower in the water.

"Where are the kids?" he asked as he rubbed a thumb along her knuckles.

She sniffed again and dragged a hand beneath her nose. "With Mrs. Givens. She's back now. Pete and Carol offered to keep them, but I hated to impose, not knowing how long you would be sick."

"You could have brought them."

She snorted a laugh, then tipped back her head, heaving a sigh as she blinked back the tears. "You'd have gone crazy with them underfoot, or scared them to death with your grouchiness. I'm not sure which would have been worse."

Frowning, he dropped his gaze to their joined hands and watched his thumb's slow movement across her porcelain skin. "I don't like being sick."

"Who does?"

He deepened his frown, remembering how rude

he'd been, how ungrateful. "I appreciate you coming to take care of me." He glanced up at her to find her staring at him. "You don't have to stay, though. I'll be all right."

He watched her eyes fill with tears again. "I want to stay and take care of you. I—" She caught her lower lip between her teeth, then slipped from the side of the tub to kneel beside it, drawing his hand to her cheek. "I'm sorry I made you angry when I asked you to leave. That wasn't my intent."

"What was it, then?" he asked gruffly, feeling the sting of her rejection all over again.

She dipped her head and drew their joined hands to her forehead, her stance almost prayerful. "I didn't want y'all to fight anymore," she murmured, "and that was the only way I could think to end it." She lifted her head, her eyes filled with tears again. "I didn't want you to leave, Clayton. Not permanently. I just wanted the fighting to stop."

"Couldn't you have just told your parents to leave?"

She sputtered a laugh. "Do you think Mother would have left with *you* still there?"

He frowned, realizing the truth in her statement.

"Clayton," she said, squeezing his hand between hers. "I want us to try again. I want us to try to make our marriage work."

"You mean it?" he asked, afraid to let himself hope.

"Yes," she said, smiling through a bright sheen of tears.

"You'll sell the place in Salado and move back here to the ranch?"

Her smile slowly faded. "Move back here?"

"This is our home," he told her, feeling the panic nudging at his chest. The only home he'd ever had. It represented the only bit of security he'd ever known.

"Yes, but..."

"But what?" he asked, lifting his gaze to keep his eyes riveted on hers as she slowly pushed to her feet. When she dropped her gaze from his, his gut tightened, fearing he was going to lose her all over again. "We don't have to talk about this now," he said quickly. "There'll be time later to work out all the details."

She drew in a deep breath, then lifted her face and smiled, though the smile looked a little forced to Clayton. "Sure," she said, and gave his hand another squeeze before releasing it. "Plenty of time. I'll see if I can find something for you to eat," she said as she turned away. "Surely Pete's left something in the pantry."

"Don't count on it," he called after her, still feeling that knot in his gut. "You know Pete. You could feed a small army with the groceries he puts away in a single day."

Clayton lay on his side, both hands tucked beneath his cheek as he stared at his sleeping wife's face. His headache had eased considerably, as had his weakness, thanks to Rena plying him with medicine and food. That knot of fear, though, remained in his gut, and he had a feeling it wasn't going to go away anytime soon. Not until he and Rena finished discussing their future living arrangements.

He knew it would sound selfish, childish even, for him to insist on them living at the ranch. But the thought of giving the place up, leaving it and moving to that rundown house Rena had bought in Salado was a possibility he couldn't even bring himself to think about. The ranch represented the only home he'd ever known, the roots he'd never had while growing up. The thought of leaving it, losing the sense of permanence it had provided him, filled him with bone-chilling fear. He was afraid he would never be able to reproduce it, would never know again that sense of security it had provided him.

Too, he had the years of work he'd put into it. The savings he'd plunked down in order to buy the place. The months on the road, chasing rodeos, in order to meet the high mortgage payments. The comfort it gave him when he was away, knowing that he had a home to return to. The satisfaction he'd felt each time he'd driven through the front gate and saw the house standing there as if waiting for him, his family tucked safely inside.

But he wondered if he could explain to Rena his feelings. Wondered whether, if he did manage to find the words, she would even understand his feeling of desperation, his need for permanence and roots.

His mind was so focused on his thoughts that he didn't realize Rena had awakened and was staring at him, her brown eyes filled with concern, until he felt the warmth of her hand settle on his cheek.

"Is your head hurting again?" she asked softly.

He pulled a hand from beneath his cheek to cover hers. "No. Just thinkin'."

"What about?"

"The ranch." He smiled ruefully. "Do you re-member when we bought it?"

Her lips curved into a soft smile of remembrance.

"Yes. It was spring and the pastures were covered with bluebonnets. We propped the twins up in the middle of a large patch and took their picture."

He chuckled, recalling the event. "We wanted to take their picture but we never got Brittany still long enough to snap the shot."

She laughed and snuggled close against his chest. "She was busy picking all the flowers and trying to eat them."

Unconscious of the movement, he dragged his other hand from beneath his cheek and shifted, drawing Rena's head to his shoulder. "And feeding them to her brother, too," he reminded her as he smoothed a hand down her hair. Stopping his hand at the base of her neck, he raised his head to look down at her. "Why did you cut your hair?"

She shrugged self-consciously. "A midlife crisis, I guess."

He snorted and rested his head by hers again. "At twenty-six? Kind of early for a midlife crisis."

She lifted a shoulder. "Maybe it was more an act of rebellion, then."

"And what were you rebelling against?" he asked, smiling as he smoothed a thumb along her jaw.

"My life. I wasn't very happy at the time, and I was desperate to do something, anything, that made me feel in control."

His smile melted as he stared down at her, knowing that he was partially responsible for her unhappiness. "You always had control, Rena. I never meant for you feel that you didn't."

She sighed, then tipped her face up to look at him. "I know you didn't, but the feeling was there just the same." She laid her cheek against his shoulder again and smoothed a hand across his chest, her gaze on her hand's slow movement. "I never experienced independence. I know that probably sounds ridiculous to you, but I never lived on my own or made my own decisions. I always did what my parents expected and wanted me to do...other than marrying you, of course," she added, glancing up at him over her brow.

He tightened his arm around her, and she sighed, returning to her stroking. "I slipped from living my life under my parents' control to living my life under yours."

"Rena," he said, his voice holding a note warning.

"No, it's true," she said, not giving him an opportunity to deny her claim. "Well, sort of true," she admitted reluctantly. "But only because I allowed it. You moved me and the twins to the ranch and went right on doing what you'd always done, while I stayed right here and filled my days taking care of them and missing you."

Hearing her say that she'd missed him touched something deep in Clayton's soul, and he drew her head to his lips and pressed a kiss against her hair. "I missed you, too," he murmured.

She glanced up at him. "You did?"

"Well, sure I did," he said, frowning.

"But you never told me that you did. Not once."

Ashamed that he hadn't, he tucked her head beneath his chin and held her there. "I guess there were a lot of things I didn't tell you."

"Yes," she said slowly. "But I realize now that there were a lot of things I never told you, either."

"Like what?"

"That I was unhappy. That I wanted you at home with us more often."

Clayton remained silent, knowing that even if she'd made her wishes known to him, it wouldn't have changed things. He still would have stayed away. He wondered if she would understand the fear that had kept him from home, and sighed when he realized he'd never know unless he found the guts to tell her. "I was scared to come home," he said quietly.

She pressed a hand against his chest to push herself up and stare down at him. "Scared? Of what?"

Unsure that he could explain his feelings, and especially not with her looking at him so intently, he tugged her back down to his side. "I never had a family. Didn't know how I was supposed to act, what I was supposed to do." He lifted a shoulder. "It was easier to stay away than chance failing."

"Oh, Clayton," she murmured, wrapping her arm around him and holding him close. "You wouldn't have failed us."

"I not only would've, I did. If I hadn't, you wouldn't have left me in the first place."

She sat up again, bracing a hand against his chest, then dragged it to hold it over his heart. "I didn't think you loved me. I thought you didn't care anything for me. And I was so lonely, so miserable without you. I finally reached the point where I knew that I had to leave, that I couldn't continue to live with things the way they were."

"See?" he said, his voice rough with regret as he closed his hand over hers. "I did fail you, when all along I thought I was avoiding failure by staying away."

Because what he said was true, Rena could think of nothing to say in return. Yet she didn't want to waste this moment, this opportunity to build a new foundation from the secrets they'd shared, the revelations they'd uncovered. Lowering her face over his, she pressed her mouth to his. "Love me, Clayton," she murmured against his lips. "Love me now."

Nine

The next morning Rena smoothed Calamine lotion over Clayton's back and smiled at the small groan of pleasure he made. "That feel good?" she asked.

"Better 'n sex."

She laughed and slapped a hand against his bare bottom, the only place free of blisters. "I think I've just been insulted."

He rolled to his back and grinned up at her. "Not necessarily. It's just that my memories are dim. Want to freshen them up a little?"

Rena pursed her lips and screwed the lid back onto the bottle of lotion. "You're sick. Remember?"

"Not that sick," he said, and waggled a brow.

Laughing, Rena leaned over and dropped a kiss on his mouth, then squealed, arms flailing, when he grabbed her and pulled her down on top of him. He locked his arms around her, holding her against him, his smile slowly fading as he looked deeply into her eyes. He lifted his head from the pillow to capture her mouth with his, but dropped it back to the pillow when the phone beside the bed rang. "Why'd you plug the damn thing back in?" he complained.

Laughing, she dropped a quick kiss on his mouth. "Because we have children," she reminded him, "and they might need us."

She stretched a hand out to snag the phone from its base. "Hello?" she said, settling back over Clayton's chest, then frowned when she heard the tears in Brittany's voice.

"Honey, what's wrong?" she asked, immediately concerned.

Clayton reached for the phone, but Rena slapped his hand away. "I know you want to see your daddy, Brittany," she said patiently, then rolled her eyes at Clayton when Brittany began to wail. "Honey," she said, raising her voice to make herself heard over her daughter's crying, "listen to me. Daddy's sick, and he doesn't feel very good right now. I know, I know," she said, pressing her fingertips against her temple as Brittany's wails turned to heartbreaking sobs. "You miss your daddy. And he misses you," she said, rubbing a hand across Clayton's bare chest as she smiled down at him. "But you're just going to have to be patient," she told Brittany. "Daddy needs a little more time to get well."

Clayton lifted a hand to cover the mouthpiece. "Go and get 'em," he whispered. "I'm not so sick that I don't want to see my kids."

"Are you sure?" she asked doubtfully. "With them here, you won't get a moment's rest. Brittany will see to that," she added pointedly.

Clayton chuckled and dropped his hand from the phone. "Go and get 'em. We can compare spots."

Laughing softly, Rena angled the receiver back to her mouth. "Brittany? Brittany, honey, if you'll quit crying for a minute, I have good news." She waited a moment, then said, "Daddy says it's okay for me to come and get you and Brandon. Put Mrs. Givens on the phone so that I can talk to her, okay?"

"Drive carefully."

Rena smiled at Clayton as she opened the front door. "I will."

He watched her walk to her Navigator, feeling as if his heart was being tugged right out of his chest and being dragged along behind her. "Rena!" he called as she opened the vehicle's door.

She stopped and turned, still smiling as she squinted her eyes against the bright sunlight. "What?"

"Give some thought to living at the ranch." He watched her smile fade and could have kicked himself for even making the suggestion.

"Why don't you give some thought to living in Salado?" she returned, then climbed into the Navigator and shut the door. Clayton watched her drive away, one hand lifted in farewell, then with a sigh he stepped back inside the house, wondering when he'd ever learn to keep his mouth shut.

Clayton lay on his stomach across the bed, his chin propped on his crossed wrists, thrumming his fingers against the mattress. He glanced at the clock for the fourth time in less than five minutes, then swore and reached for the phone. It rang before he had a chance to pick it up.

Snatching the receiver from the base, he said, "Rena?", praying it was her on the other end of the line.

"Yes, it's me," she replied, sounding tired.

"Where are you?"

"At home. In Salado," she added.

His heart stuttered a beat. "Is something wrong?"

"Several somethings. I'm not going to be able to bring the children back tonight. The hot water heater burst and flooded the upstairs. I called a plumber, but he can't get here until tomorrow."

"I'm on my way," he said, already swinging his legs over the side of the bed, prepared to do just that.

"No. You're too sick. There's no need for you to drive all the way to Salado. I can handle things here. Brittany, don't!" she cried.

His heart jumped to his throat at the alarm in her voice and he leaped to his feet. "What's the matter? Is she hurt?"

"No. She's dragging her blanket through the water. Listen, Clayton, I need to go. I've got to finish mopping up the water before it ruins the wood floors. I'll call you tomorrow."

Before he could say anything, there was a click in his ear. He sank back down on the bed, disappointment weighing on his shoulders. With a frown he leaned to drop the receiver on its base, then fell back on the bed. He groaned as the sheets scratched across his sores, and rolled to his stomach, propping his chin on his wrists again.

He was tempted to ignore Rena's claim that she could handle things without his help and hightail it for Salado…but then he remembered the fervor with which she had told him of her desire to feel independent and in control.

He'd give her twenty-four hours to resolve her plumbing problems, he promised himself. But if she wasn't home by then, he was heading to Salado whether she thought she needed his help or not.

Sick to death of being closed up indoors for so long, Clayton stepped out onto the front porch. He stretched his arms high above his head, growled low in his throat, then dropped his arms to his sides with a sigh. Deciding this was the perfect spot to watch for Rena and the twins' arrival, he dragged one of the wicker chairs close to the railing. With a glance at the front door, to reassure himself he'd left it open and could hear the phone if it rang, he dropped down on the chair and lifted his feet, propping his boots on the low railing.

With his hands folded behind his head, he leaned back and waited, his gaze on the long drive that stretched from the house to the main road. He could see Pete in the distance, riding his horse, and kind of hoped Pete would head his way. He was tired of his own company and thought jawing with Pete for a while might help pass the time while he waited for Rena and the kids to arrive.

He narrowed his eyes as a car turned onto the drive, then dropped his arms and stood, waiting for the car to reach the house. When it did, a man stepped from the vehicle, pausing a moment to adjust a gray felt cowboy hat over his head, before turning for the house.

Clayton noted the county sheriff's emblem on the

side of the door, the badge on the man's shirt, and his blood ran cold. "What can I do for you?" he called out.

The man stopped and looked up at him. "Are you Clayton Rankin?"

"Yessir, I am," Clayton replied and crossed to the steps.

The man slipped a sheaf of papers from the inside of his jacket and handed them to Clayton. "Consider yourself served," he said, then touched a finger to the brim of his hat in farewell and strode back to his car.

Stunned, Clayton looked down at the papers he held, knowing without looking what they were. Suddenly weak-kneed, he sank down to the steps.

"Hey, Clayton!"

Clayton glanced up, his eyes narrowed dangerously, and watched Pete lope his horse toward the house, then rein him to a sudden stop not more than three feet from the steps.

"You in trouble with the law or something?" Pete teased as he swung a leg over the back of the saddle and dropped to the ground.

"You might say so," Clayton muttered. He held out the papers to Pete. "Seems I've just been served."

Frowning, Pete took the papers and opened them. He scanned the first few lines, then murmured, "Oh, man. This is bad. Real bad. I didn't think she was going to go through with it."

"Seems she not only *was,* she did." Clayton rose and snatched the papers from Pete's hand, then turned and headed for the front door.

"What are you going to do?" Pete called, stopping him.

"Do?" Clayton replied, turning. "Find me a rodeo. What else?"

Rena drove up to the house and parked, frowning at the dark windows. Though it was late, she thought Clayton would have waited up for her. "Come on, kids," she said, stretching over the back seat to unbuckle their seat belts. "Let's go and wake up Daddy."

Before Rena could open her own door, the twins were jumping to the ground and running, screaming, "Daddy! We're home!"

Chuckling, Rena closed her door and followed them, watching as they burst through the front door, and silently prayed that Clayton was feeling up to a full-scale invasion. Knowing he wouldn't have a choice in the matter, not with the twins so anxious to see him, she stepped across the threshold, switching on a light. She could hear the twins running down the hall, arguing over who got to wake up their daddy. She sighed, tossed her purse to a chair and followed, prepared to rescue him, if necessary.

The twins met her in the hallway, their faces downcast.

"What's wrong?" she asked. "Where's your daddy?"

"He's not here," Brittany complained.

Rena glanced over their heads to peer at the dark doorway of the master bedroom. "Are you sure?"

"We looked everywhere. Do you think maybe he's at the barn?"

Though she doubted it, Rena walked back to the

kitchen, flipping on the overhead light as she went to the back door. Opening it, she looked out toward the barn and noticed, for the first time, that Clayton's truck was missing. "Maybe he had to go into town for something," she said to the twins.

"No, he didn't."

Rena jumped, a scream building in her throat, then swallowed it when Pete stepped from the shadows and into the light. "Pete Dugan!" she cried. "You should be shot! You nearly scared the life out of me."

"Sorry. But I saw the headlights from Carol's when you turned onto the drive and figured I better make sure someone wasn't sneaking in to clear out the place." He narrowed an eye at her. "That wasn't your plan, was it?"

"What plan?" Rena asked in confusion.

"To clean the house out while Clayton's gone."

"Gone?" she repeated, even more confused. "Where? And why would I want to clean out the house?"

He folded his arms across his chest, and lifted a shoulder. "Heard of women doing that. Grabbing all they can before the divorce is final."

"Divorce?" Rena echoed. "We're not getting a divorce."

"I don't know what kind of game you're playin'," Pete said, "but I'm gettin' a little tired of being strung along."

Glancing down to see the twins hanging on every word, Rena put a hand on a shoulder of each and turned them from the door. "Y'all go watch TV for a minute," she said, and gave them a little nudge in that direction, "while I talk to Pete."

When she was sure they were out of earshot, she turned back to Pete. "I don't know what Clayton has told you," she said tersely, "but I have *not* filed for a divorce."

Pete lifted his chin, gesturing inside the house and to the kitchen table. "Somebody did. The papers are there are on the table. Saw 'em myself."

Rena spun, saw the sheaf of carefully folded papers on the table, then bolted for them, snatching them up and holding them open, her fingers trembling. She scanned the first page, flipped to the next, then quickly shuffled to the last page. "Ben Wheeler," she muttered furiously, crumpling the papers in her fist.

"Who's Ben Wheeler?" Pete asked, having followed her into the kitchen.

"My father's attorney," she said, spinning to face him. "Do you know where Clayton is?"

"Not far. Seguine."

"Will you stay with the children?"

"Why? Where are you goin'?"

"I'm going after my husband."

Pete ripped off his hat with a loud whoop and tossed it to the table. "'Atta girl! Throw a rope around him and drag him home!"

Anxious to escape the bright lights and the questioning glances, Clayton put his spurs to Easy's sides, urging the horse into a trot as he headed for his trailer. If one more person asked him if he'd managed to talk Rena into coming back home with him, he was afraid he was going to put a fist through somebody's face. Mainly Pete's, since he suspected it was Pete who had broadcast Clayton's personal business for all the world to know.

Reining his horse to a stop beside the trailer, he slid down from the saddle and flipped the rein over Easy's head.

"Do you believe everything you read?"

Clayton whipped his head around at the sound of Rena's voice, his heart stopping for a minute, then scowled and turned away, tying Easy's reins to the side of the trailer. "When it's delivered by a sheriff and written up by some fancy lawyer, I do."

"That's a shame," she said, and stepped from the shadows to stand at the opposite side of Easy's head. "If you hadn't, you would have been home to greet me and the children when we arrived."

His fingers faltered a moment, but he forced them back into motion, jerking the reins into a slip knot.

Rena laid a hand against the horse's nose and rubbed. "Hello, Easy," she murmured. "You did really well tonight."

Clayton jerked his head around to stare at her. "You saw me make my throw?"

Her gaze on the horse, Rena smiled. "Yes. It was a good one, though you were a little slow coming out of the box."

Hell, yeah, I was a little slow, Clayton thought angrily. Anybody who'd been served divorce papers not more than five hours before, would have been a little distracted. Scowling, he lifted the saddle's fender and hooked the stirrup over the horn. "Maybe so," he said sourly, "but I'm in the lead."

Rena cut a glance his way. "The rodeo's not over yet."

Clayton gave the girth strap a tug, releasing it, then

pulled the sweaty strap through the ring. "You here to critique my ropin'?"

She ducked under the horse's head to stand beside Clayton. "No, I came to take you home."

Suddenly feeling light-headed, Clayton braced an arm against the saddle and leaned into it, pressing his forehead into the curve of his elbow.

Rena stepped closer and placed a hand lightly against his back. "I didn't send those papers, Clayton," she said softly. "My father did."

He gulped a breath, afraid he was going to cry, but kept his face buried against his arm, not wanting her to see his tears if he did. "You didn't know anything about it?"

"No. Not a thing. Which, I assure you, is a matter I will take up with my father first thing in the morning."

She rubbed her hand up his back and curled her fingers around his neck. "I love you, Clayton," she said softly and drew his head to meet hers. "We're going to get through this. I promise you. Somehow we're going to get through this."

He turned then, and hauled her into his arms, burying his face against her hair. "God, Rena," he cried, squeezing her tight enough to crack bone. "I've never been so scared in my life. I don't want to lose you. I'd die if I lost you. You're my life. My everything."

As quickly as he'd grabbed her, he released her, only to catch her cheeks between his hands. "I love you, Rena," he whispered, his eyes gleaming with tears. "I love you with all my heart, all my soul. And I swear, I'll never stop telling you that. You'll hear those words till the day I die."

Laughing, Rena threw her arms around his neck. "Clayton! You said it. You finally said it!"

Laughing with her, he lifted her from her feet and spun her around. "I love you, I love you, I love you," he yelled for all the world to hear.

"Do *me*, Daddy! Do *me!*"

Clayton stumbled to a stop and slowly lowered Rena back to her feet. Both of them turned to find Pete standing behind them, a twin propped on each hip, Brittany with her arms outstretched to her daddy.

Pete lifted both shoulders and grinned. "I said no a thousand times or more. Every time they asked me to bring them over here, I said no. I swear I did. I probably could've held out a little longer, despite the pressure they were puttin' on me, but then one started squallin', then the other one tuned up." He lifted his shoulders again. "Hell, what's a man supposed to do?"

"Uh-oh," Brittany said, clamping a hand over her mouth and giggling. "You said a no-no word, Uncle Pete."

Clayton walked over and slapped a hand down on the brim of Pete's hat, knocking it down over his eyes. "He sure did, shortcake," he said, and plucked Brittany from Pete's arm and shifted her to his hip. "Guess he'll have to spend some time in the time-out chair."

Rena held out her arms, and Brandon fell into them. "Sure will," she agreed, planting Brandon on her hip. "Or we could just wash his mouth with soap."

"Now there's an idea," Clayton said as he wrapped his arm around Rena's waist. He headed her toward his truck. "In fact, I think I've got a bar of lye soap in my trailer.

"Hey, now, wait a minute," Pete complained, shoving his hat back on his head and bracing his hands on his hips as he stared after them. "Isn't a man entitled to a trial before he's proclaimed guilty and hung?"

Rena and Clayton both turned to look back at him. "Hung?" they said in unison, then turned to look at each other. "Hung," Clayton said again, arching a questioning brow at his wife.

Rena considered the possibility a moment. "No," she said, shaking her head. "Better not hang him. Carol would never forgive us."

"Well, thank you for that small kindness," Pete said grumpily, and started after them. "And after I hauled these kids all the way over here, too, thinkin' y'all might need a little help in ironin' out your problems. Havin' to stop four times for pit stops along the way. Twice for burgers and fries. Hellfire!"

He stopped when Rena and Clayton both turned on him again, then he held up a hand and started backing up. "Now wait a minute. That was just a slip of the tongue. I didn't mean to say hellfire. I meant to say shoot. Yeah, that's it. Shoot."

When Clayton continued to frown at him, Pete dragged off his hat and lifted his head, sniffin' the air. "Do you smell what I smell?"

"What do you smell, Uncle Pete?" Brittany asked.

"Cotton candy. Mmm-mmm. Don't it just make your taste buds stand up at attention and cry for some that sweet spun sugar?"

"I smell it, too," Brittany cried. "Can I have some, Daddy? Please?"

"Me, too," Brandon chimed in.

Clayton frowned at Pete. "Mighty fancy footwork," he said as he set the squirming Brittany down on her feet.

Pete just grinned and took both Brittany and Brandon by a hand. "Yep. Pulled myself out of tighter scrapes than this one. In fact, I remember doing some mighty fast talkin' for your daddy one time," Pete began as he led the twins away. "We were in this country and western dance hall in Oklahoma City, and there was this blonde your daddy had the hots for—"

"Pete!" Clayton and Rena cried in unison.

He glanced over his shoulder and grinned. "Ya'll remember that one, too, huh?" He chuckled. "Don't worry. I'll give 'em the Walt Disney version of the night y'all met."

Rena and Clayton turned to look at each other.

"Surely he wouldn't—" Rena began.

"Nah," Clayton said, and looped his arms around her waist, drawing her abdomen to his. "Not even Pete's that crazy." He dipped his head to drop a kiss on her lips, then slid his hands down to cup her buttocks. "We got more than we bargained for that night, but I have no regrets. Do you?"

"No," she said, lifting her arms to wrap around his neck. "Though we still have to discuss where we're going to live."

"Now I've been thinking about that," Clayton said, leaning back to look down at her. "And I've come to realize that I had developed a false notion that the ranch represented home to me."

Rena furrowed her brow in confusion. "But it was our home."

"Yeah," he agreed. "It was. But what I realized was that it wasn't the *place* that signified home. It was *you*. And I want you to know that if you've got your heart set on living in that falling-down house in Salado, then that's where I'm hanging my hat, too."

"Do you mean it, Clayton?" she asked hopefully.

"Damn straight. In fact, I think we need to get busy and make us some more babies. There are a lot of empty rooms in that old house."

"How about right now?"

He glanced around, then dropped his gaze back to hers. "Right now?"

She pulled her arms from around his neck and grabbed his hand, tugging him along behind her. "You've still got that bed in the loft of your trailer, don't you?"

"Well, yeah," he said, casting a nervous glance over his shoulder. "But what about the kids?"

She stopped beside the trailer and rose to her toes to drape her arms around his neck again. "Pete can handle the kids," she said, and began to nibble at his lower lip. "And, if he can't…well, Pete's a pretty sharp guy. He'll figure something out to keep them entertained."

Epilogue

At the sound of a sniffle, Clayton slipped his arm around Rena's waist and drew her reassuringly against his side. She glanced up at him, her eyes brimming with tears.

"He looks so happy, doesn't he?" she whispered.

Clayton glanced toward the beaming groom and his very pregnant bride, who were making their way back up the aisle of the church, then down at his wife and smiled. "Yeah, he does."

Pete leaned from the pew behind them, sticking his face between Rena's and Clayton's and forcing their heads apart. "You'd think after marrying Shelby *three* times," he muttered irritably, "that some of Troy's jubilation would have worn off by now."

Frowning, Clayton planted a hand against Pete's

face and gave him a shove, then drew Rena back to his side and smiled down at her. "Sometimes there's more to celebrate the second and third time around, isn't there sweetheart?"

Rena leaned into him, her eyes filled with love for her husband. "I can't speak for the third time around, but I certainly found much more to celebrate about the second time we exchanged marriage vows."

Remembering the vows of renewal they'd repeated just two weeks before, Clayton felt his heart squeeze in his chest. "Yeah," he murmured and dipped his head over Rena's, pressing a kiss to her lips. "So did I."

Brittany climbed up onto the pew and squirmed her way between her parents. "I want a kiss, too, Daddy," she complained jealously.

Laughing, Clayton scooped his daughter up into his arms. "Sure thing, shortcake." He popped her a kiss square on the mouth, then leaned back to look at her. "How was that?"

She pushed her lips out into a pout. "You kissed Mommy longer than you kissed me."

Chuckling, Clayton shifted her to his opposite hip and drew Rena back against his side. "That's because Mommy's my wife and you're my little girl."

He felt a tug on his sleeve and glanced down to find Brandon peering up at him. His son held up his arms to him. Smiling, Clayton hooked an arm around Brandon's waist and hefted him up to his hip. "What's the matter, cowboy? You feeling left out?"

"No," Brandon replied and leaned to peer over his daddy's shoulder. "But everybody's leavin'."

Clayton glanced around and noticed that the wedding guests were filing out of the church. ''Guess we better be headin' out, too.''

As he stepped out into the aisle, Pete snatched Brittany from his arms, handed her off to Carol, then took Brandon from him, hitched him on his hip and took off after Carol.

''Hey!'' Clayton called after them. ''Where are y'all going with my kids?''

Pete glanced back over his shoulder, grinning. ''Thought I might give 'em a few pointers on the art of rice throwin''''

Rena slipped her arm through Clayton's. ''Do you think we should warn Troy and Shelby of the coming attack?'' she asked uneasily.

Clayton glanced down at her and grinned. ''And ruin all the fun?''

She laughed and slipped her arms around his waist, tipping up her face to peer at him. ''I love you, Clayton Rankin.''

''No more than I love you, sweetheart.''

With a sigh of contentment, she rested her cheek against his chest. ''Clayton?''

Sure that he'd never grow tired of telling his wife how much he loved her or of hearing her declare her love for him, he hummed a lazy response. ''Hmm?''

''Were you serious about wanting to fill our house in Salado with more children?''

Puzzled by the hesitancy he heard in her voice, he leaned back to look down at her. ''Sure I was serious. Why?''

She dropped her gaze to his chest and drew a small circle on the front of his shirt with her fingernail.

"Well..." she lifted her head. "I think in about eight months you'll get your wish."

Clayton stared at her a moment before her meaning set in. "You mean..."

She nodded her head, her lips trembling in a smile. "Yes, I mean."

He wrapped his arms around her and hugged her tightly against him. "A baby," he murmured, then said again awed by the thought. "A baby."

"Clayton?"

He nuzzled his nose against her hair. "What, sweetheart?"

"Better make that babies."

He froze, his eyes flipping wide, his nose still buried in her hair. "Twins?"

Her hair rubbed against the side of his face in silent ascent.

"Twins," he repeated, releasing a long breath.

"Yes, twins," she said tearfully.

He quickly pushed her to arm's length, searching her face. "You're not upset, are you?"

"No," she said, sniffing. "Are you?"

"Heck, no!" he cried and tugged her against his chest again. He vised his arms around her, holding her close, then just as quickly pushed her to arm's length again, his face creased with worry. "If the babies are boys, you won't name 'em Pete and Repeat, like Pete wanted you to when we had Brittany and Brandon, will you?"

Rena tossed back her head and laughed. "Not a chance."

"Thank goodness," he murmured in relief as he drew her back against his chest. Pressing a kiss to her temple, he sighed, his heart swelling with the love he felt for his wife—a love that he would never again take for granted, and a love he would cherish always.

* * * * *

Look for Peggy Moreland's next book,

THE WAY TO A RANCHER'S HEART,

*coming to Silhouette Desire
in February 2001!*

July 2000
BACHELOR DOCTOR
#1303 by Barbara Boswell

August 2000
THE RETURN OF ADAMS CADE
#1309 by BJ James
Men of Belle Terre

September 2000
SLOW WALTZ ACROSS TEXAS
#1315 by Peggy Moreland
Texas Grooms

October 2000
THE DAKOTA MAN
#1321 by Joan Hohl

November 2000
HER PERFECT MAN
#1328 by Mary Lynn Baxter

December 2000
IRRESISTIBLE YOU
#1333 by Barbara Boswell

MAN OF THE MONTH

For twenty years Silhouette has been giving
you the ultimate in romantic reads. Come join
some of your favorite authors in helping us to
celebrate our anniversary with the most rugged,
sexy and lovable heroes ever!

Available at your favorite retail outlet.

Silhouette®
Where love comes alive™

Celebrate Silhouette Books' 20th anniversary
with a sizzler from beloved author

ANNETTE BROADRICK
Marriage Prey

Love is in the air when the families from
HUNTER'S PREY and **BACHELOR FATHER**—
Annette Broadrick's first two Silhouette Desire
novels—are brought together under
explosive circumstances!

Mesmerized by her beauty and innocence,
Steve Antonelli rescued stranded Robin McAlister and
welcomed her to his island hideaway. The vivacious
virgin was much too young for this world-weary
homicide detective, but her yearning kisses beckoned
him to fulfill her every fantasy. However, never in his
wildest dreams did Steve predict their unforgettable
romantic interlude would result in a shotgun wedding!

Available at your favorite retail outlet.

Silhouette®
Where love comes alive™

***Don't miss
an exciting opportunity
to save on the purchase of
Harlequin and Silhouette books!***

Buy any two Harlequin or
Silhouette books and save
$10.00 off future Harlequin
and Silhouette purchases

OR

buy any three
Harlequin or Silhouette books
and save **$20.00 off** future
Harlequin and Silhouette purchases.

***Watch for details
coming in October 2000!***

PHQ400

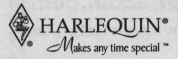

HARLEQUIN®
Makes any time special ™

Silhouette®
Where love comes alive ™

If you enjoyed what you just read,
then we've got an offer you can't resist!

Take 2 bestselling love stories FREE!

Plus get a FREE surprise gift!

Clip this page and mail it to Silhouette Reader Service™

IN U.S.A.
3010 Walden Ave.
P.O. Box 1867
Buffalo, N.Y. 14240-1867

IN CANADA
P.O. Box 609
Fort Erie, Ontario
L2A 5X3

YES! Please send me 2 free Silhouette Desire® novels and my free surprise gift. Then send me 6 brand-new novels every month, which I will receive months before they're available in stores. In the U.S.A., bill me at the bargain price of $3.34 plus 25¢ delivery per book and applicable sales tax, if any*. In Canada, bill me at the bargain price of $3.74 plus 25¢ delivery per book and applicable taxes**. That's the complete price and a savings of at least 10% off the cover prices—what a great deal! I understand that accepting the 2 free books and gift places me under no obligation ever to buy any books. I can always return a shipment and cancel at any time. Even if I never buy another book from Silhouette, the 2 free books and gift are mine to keep forever. So why not take us up on our invitation. You'll be glad you did!

225 SEN C222
326 SEN C223

Name	(PLEASE PRINT)	
Address	Apt.#	
City	State/Prov.	Zip/Postal Code

* Terms and prices subject to change without notice. Sales tax applicable in N.Y.
** Canadian residents will be charged applicable provincial taxes and GST.
  All orders subject to approval. Offer limited to one per household.
  ® are registered trademarks of Harlequin Enterprises Limited.

DES00   ©1998 Harlequin Enterprises Limited

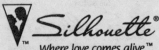

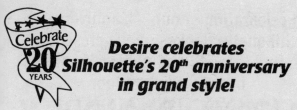

COMING NEXT MONTH

CMN0900